The Lo

Boo.

Bella's Story

Katrina Kahler

Table of Contents

CHAPTER ONE

We were right in the middle of a pop quiz in History class when the classroom phone rang. I was trying to figure out the answer to the next problem on my worksheet. Even though I'd kept up on my reading, there had been a lot of names to memorize and I was struggling with what to write.

The ringing of the phone distracted me. In fact, it distracted everyone in the room and I was aware that each pair of eyes was directed to the front. The phone rarely rang in any classroom, but when it did, it was usually to call a student to the office for one reason or another. And if the call had anything to do with the new principal, Mrs. Fletcher, that was usually not a good thing at all.

I waited along with everyone else for our teacher to finish speaking. As soon as she hung up the phone, she turned and looked directly at me. "Bella?"

One of the boys, a kid named Tommy Riggs, let out an "ooohhh" sound as if I was in trouble.

"Yes?" I replied, throwing Tommy a dirty look.

"Principal Fletcher would like to see you," Mrs. Evans said.

"Me?" I asked. "Why would she want to see me?"

A few kids snickered to themselves. But I hadn't asked the question to be rude. I was a good student. I knew I hadn't done anything wrong and I had no idea why I'd been called upon.

"Leave your test," Mrs. Evans instructed me. "You can make it up later."

I glanced at my best friend, Abbie, who sat next to me. Her blue eyes were wide with fear.

Mine were too.

"What did you do?" she mouthed.

"Nothing," I mouthed back and shrugged.

I stood up from my chair and smoothed my hands over my silky blue shirt and walked out of the classroom, trying to ignore the stares that I felt hammering into the back of my head.

In the hallway, I let out a shaky breath. Mrs. Fletcher was an intimidating woman and perhaps I'd done something wrong without realizing it. If anyone was ever called into her office, it only meant one thing…trouble.

I'd never met her face to face, but the kids who had didn't have anything good to say about her at all. There had to be some mistake. Maybe there was another Bella in the school who she'd mixed up with me.

That thought eased my mind a little. Surely, that was what had happened. I could hardly wait to see Mrs. Fletcher's embarrassment when she realized.

When I arrived at the office, one of the secretaries led me down a small hallway toward a door with Mrs. Fletcher's name on it.

"I don't understand why I'm here," I said to the secretary as we walked.

"Mrs. Fletcher will explain everything," she replied curtly then opened the door and ushered me inside.

"Bella Barlow is here to see you," the secretary announced to Principal Fletcher.

The office was stuffy and boring. There were portraits on the wall of people I didn't know and there wasn't one bright color to be seen. The only furniture was a desk and two chairs in front of it.

In one of the chairs sat another woman. I had no idea who she was. I had never seen her before, but she stood up the moment the door closed behind me.
Glancing back, I saw that the secretary was gone. It seemed that even she was afraid of Mrs. Fletcher.

"Please, take a seat," Mrs. Fletcher said.

Her hair was tied back, not a strand out of place. Her red lips were usually frowning whenever I saw her stalking the hallways or at school assemblies. But today, they were pursed in a way I'd never seen before.

What was this all about?

"I'm Mrs. Williams," the other woman said, opening her hand to me.

I shook it, and she led me to the chair next to hers.

"I'm a social worker," she said. "Do you know what that is?"

My throat constricted tightly and I struggled to breathe. Something was wrong. What did she want with me? Social workers were important people. Surely if there was a problem, my mom or dad would be there too.

"What's going on?" I asked, my voice sounding like it belonged to a squeaky mouse.

Mrs. Williams looked at Mrs. Fletcher who nodded in encouragement.

Mrs. Williams glanced uneasily back at me before clearing her throat. Then her words poured out in a rush.

"I'm so sorry to have to bring you this news, Bella but your parents were involved in a car accident this morning."

"Are they okay?" I gasped. "Are you taking me to the hospital?"

Mrs. Williams looked at Mrs. Fletcher again. I wished she'd stop doing that.

"It was a fatal car accident," Mrs. Williams said after a few moments. "Your parents didn't survive."

The words "didn't survive" played on rewind over and over in my head. I stared back at her and gaped. Gulping down a quick breath, I opened my mouth to speak. But nothing would come out. I heard the words again...*your parents didn't survive.* What did she mean my parents didn't survive? What was she talking about?

My head began to spin as I gulped again, a rising heat filling my body and overwhelming me like a furnace.

"Wh...what did you say?"

Although I had heard her clearly, her words didn't make sense and I was praying that I'd misunderstood her after all.

She reached over to touch my arm gently as she reworded the sentence. "Apparently it was a terrible accident, Bella, and your parents were killed. I'm so sorry."

I felt as though I was floating. It was as if I'd left my body and was watching the scene below. I could see myself, sitting silent and speechless in my chair. I could see Mrs. Williams, her features filled with sympathy as she stared back. And I could see our principal, Mrs. Fletcher, her expression mirroring that of the other woman.

All of a sudden, the image seemed to fade into a dazy haze in front of me and the reality of the words finally found their mark. I shook my head in denial. There had to be some mistake. Things like this didn't happen to me, Bella Barlow, the girl who lived with her two loving parents in a pretty house at the end of Martin Street.

"Bella," Mrs. Fletcher's husky voice broke through the

fog.

I blinked as the room came into focus again. My stomach churned, and I thought I was going to be sick right then and there, all over Mrs. Fletcher's sparkling desktop, all over Mrs. Williams herself.

But then Mrs. Williams spoke again and my eyes shot to hers. "From your records," she said, lifting a thin manila envelope from her leather bag, "we've learned you have no relatives, except for two very elderly and unwell grandparents who live on the other side of the country. So there aren't any family members to take you in and care for you.

I stared back at her, unable to speak. All I could manage to do was shake my head. This could not be real. This must be a nightmare that I would wake from at any minute. It had to be.

"We've contacted the only name on your emergency contact list," she continued gently, "a woman named Sarah Barnes."

"My mom's best friend," the words popped out of my mouth, as if on auto-pilot.

Mrs. Fletcher nodded. "She will be here shortly."

I tried to process what that meant, what Mrs. Williams and Mrs. Fletcher were talking about. Sarah knew? If Sarah knew, if Sarah was coming, then this must all be real. My skin was on fire, I could hardly breathe, but at the same time, I couldn't move from my seat. I glanced at the window, desperately in need of some air.

Mrs. Fletcher's eyes remained on mine and I looked down at my hands. They were clasped tightly in my lap. The nail polish on my pinkie was chipped. Mom had painted my nails the week before. And just that morning in class, we'd been informed that nail polish was now banned at school. That and any jewelry except for small stud earrings were no longer allowed. It was a new rule that Mrs. Fletcher had enforced. No more nail polish. And no more jewelry. The thought swam in my head as I stared at my fingers, wondering why I was even thinking about those things at a moment like this.

Tears welled in my eyes as someone knocked on the door.

Mrs. Fletcher got up from her seat and lightly squeezed my shoulder as she moved to answer it.

"Bella?" a familiar voice said a moment later.

I turned to see Sarah. Her eyes were red-rimmed and her face was flushed. Her long dark hair was tied loosely in a ponytail.

I jumped out of my chair and raced towards her.

Mrs. Fletcher moved out of the way as Sarah dropped down to her knees and hugged me.

"I'm so sorry, Little Bean," she said. The nickname she'd called me for as long as I could remember opened up the flood of tears that had been hovering just beneath the surface. I suddenly broke down into choking sobs, gripping hold of her and never wanting to let go.

"Mrs. Barnes," Mrs. Williams said from the doorway.

Sarah craned her neck to look at the social worker. "It's Ms. Barnes."

"My apologies," Mrs. Williams said, "if you don't mind, I need to speak to you privately."

I grabbed Sarah's hand. I wasn't letting her out of my sight.

Sarah squeezed my hand in return. "Whatever you have to say, you can say in front of Bella, too."

Mrs. Williams sighed. She glanced at me and then back to Sarah, before opening her mouth to explain.

"This morning around ten, a call was sent to the dispatch center. There was a two-car accident on Meyer's bridge. There was some construction, and the roads were slippery from the rain. All occupants of both cars were—" she stopped and glanced at me once again before she said the final word… "killed."

Everything faded into oblivion. I clung to Sarah, blocking out the sound of Mrs. Williams' voice. The only detail I heard was that Sarah was taking me home with her.

"This will be a temporary arrangement," Mrs. Williams said to Sarah. "I'll be in contact later today."

I hugged Sarah's waist and closed my eyes, wishing there was some possible way that I could wake up from this nightmare.

As Sarah and I left the school, the vision of saying goodbye to my parents that morning flooded my mind and I could barely walk as the world blurred right before my eyes.

CHAPTER TWO

Three Weeks Later

I was still waking up expecting to see Mom walk into my bedroom, gently nudging me awake so I could get ready for school. But instead of Mom's sweet voice, I woke to the sound of Mia, Sarah's two-year-old daughter, bouncing on her crib mattress next to my bed.

"Bella! Bella!" she chanted over and over until I finally rolled out of bed to get to her.

Even though my heart was broken, Mia made waking up just a bit easier. Her crooked smile made me smile, and I held onto a little hope that everything would turn out okay.

I tried to focus on the thought of Mrs. Williams making the "temporary" living arrangement with Sarah a permanent thing. Although I knew she was searching for a foster family to take me in, I pushed that thought aside. I was determined that was not going to happen. I was going to stay with Sarah.

Sarah brushed Mrs. Williams off whenever she called by or phoned to check on me. But with two other kids to care for and a full-time job, I wasn't sure Mrs. Williams thought Sarah would be able to look after me too.

Then one night, close to dinnertime, Mrs. Williams arrived at Sarah's apartment. I recognized the sound of the two rapid knocks on the door. It was the way she always knocked when she came over.

"Keep stirring the sauce," Sarah said before jogging out to the living room to answer the door.

I turned down the heat on the stove and sneaked away, wanting to listen to what Mrs. Williams had to say. Even though I was determined to stay with Sarah and her young children, I lived with a fear that Mrs. Williams would force me to live somewhere else. And each time I heard her knock, I wondered if she had arrived to take me away.

"We're still searching for a family," Mrs. Williams said from the other room.

I put a hand on my chest, letting out a big breath.

"You can call on the phone with these updates, you know," Sarah said. "Every time Bella sees you, I have to calm her down afterward. Can't you see she's distressed?"

Peering into the living room, I could see that Sarah had her arms crossed and she wasn't moving from her spot. Mrs. Williams stood on the small rug by the door, and it didn't look like Sarah was going to invite her in.

"I need to make sure that Bella is well cared for," Mrs. Williams said as she took in the room behind Sarah.

Sure, there were toys everywhere, but what did she expect? Sarah had two little kids, of course there would be toys lying around. I helped Sarah cook and clean. Living with her wasn't going to be easy, but I knew how to help out.

"Hopefully we'll find a suitable foster family soon," Mrs. Williams said.

Sarah sighed and rubbed her forehead with the palm of her hand.

Why wasn't Sarah fighting for me?

I came out from my hiding spot and stormed into the room. If she wasn't going to fight for me, I would do it myself. "Why can't I stay with Sarah?"

Sarah whipped around; her eyes wide as if I'd startled her. "Bella, I asked you—"

"I don't want to live with another family," I said to Mrs. Williams. "I like it here. I want to stay here with Sarah and Mia and …."

Mrs. Williams shook her head. "I'm sorry, Bella. But there are rules. Ms. Barnes has a lot to cope with already."

I looked at Sarah. She was frowning.

"This apartment is too small for three children, and unfortunately Sarah isn't your legal guardian. It's not possible to make this a permanent home for you."

Tears streaked down my face. "But a foster family? They'll be strangers! Why do I have to live with strangers? What about my grandparents? Why can't I stay with them?"

My grandparents were very old and lived on the other side of the country, but they were a better option than staying with a family I didn't even know.

Mrs. William side-stepped Sarah and walked into the room, closer to me. She sat down on the ottoman, sliding one of Mia's toys aside. "Bella, we've already gone over this. Your grandparents are elderly and unwell. Your grandmother has just been relocated to a nursing home and neither of your grandparents is fit to care for a twelve-year-old girl."

"I don't want to leave here," I said softly.

"I think that's enough for tonight," Sarah said, opening the front door again. Her message was clear, she wanted Mrs. Williams out of her home and so did I. "Please call next time instead of just showing up. You're not helping the situation."

Mrs. Williams patted my shoulder and then stood up. "I'll be in touch."

Once the door closed with Mrs. Williams on the other side, Sarah came over to me and wiped a tear from my cheek. "Let's finish making dinner before Mia wakes from her nap."

Every day after that, each little sound at the door made me jump. But Mrs. Williams didn't show up or call Sarah with any news. I wondered if there was a shortage of foster families. Then I'd be able to stay with Sarah after all. Sarah had always been like a second mom to me, and I loved both her children. Having me live there with Matthew and Mia didn't seem like a strain on anyone. We all got along and it was perfect.

Why would Mrs. Williams purposefully take me out of a good situation just because Sarah's place was too small? It didn't make sense to me.

One morning while Sarah was making breakfast, someone knocked on the door.

Sarah had a pan of scrambled eggs on the stove, and she looked at me. "Can you grab the door please, Bella?"

"Sure," I said, sliding out from my seat. I shoved the piece of toast I was holding into my mouth and went to the front door.

With no word from Mrs. Williams for several days, I'd started to relax and was certainly not expecting her to visit. She hadn't knocked in her usual manner so I was quite unprepared. Seeing her standing there almost made me choke on my breakfast.

"Bella, good morning. You're just the girl I want to see," she said.

She seemed so happy that I was sure she must have good news and was about to tell Sarah and me that I could stay.

"Come in," I said.

She moved into the living room and glanced into the kitchen where Sarah was busy with Mia and Matthew.

"I know this isn't what you wanted, but—"

My jaw dropped open, realizing instantly what she was about to say.

It was not the news I'd been hoping for.

It was the worst news ever.

CHAPTER THREE

"Bella? Did you hear what I said?" Mrs. Williams prompted.

I blinked, the living room coming into sharper focus. I backed away from her, kicking over one of Matthew's Lego castles.

Mrs. Williams misunderstood my reaction and smiled as if she'd just won some competition.

"We've found you a lovely home with two excellent parents. They have more than enough space, and they also have two children, a girl around your age and a younger boy as well. I know how great you are with young kids. This family is perfect for you. They will take care of you, and I'm sure you'll be very happy there."

I shook my head, unwilling to accept what she was saying.

"Bella!" Sarah called from the other room. "Who is it?"

"It's just me," Mrs. Williams called out.

Sarah entered the living room, wiping her hands on a small gray towel. "Mrs. Williams. We weren't expecting you." She tucked a stray strand of hair into her bun.

Sarah came to my side and stood next to me. "Would you like a cup of coffee?"

Mrs. Williams smiled, but she seemed a little nervous now that Sarah was in the room. "No, thank you. I was just telling Bella that I've found a family for her."

Sarah stiffened. She hadn't been expecting this news either.

Mrs. Williams went on to tell Sarah the same things she'd told me. Even though she repeated the same words, I still could not accept them.

Did Mrs. Williams really expect me to live with a family I didn't even know? I didn't care if they had two kids. I wanted to live with Sarah and her children.

"This will move rather quickly now," Mrs. Williams said. "I'll be taking Bella to her new home today."

"Today?" I repeated, my mouth falling open in shock.

Mrs. Williams nodded.

I stared back at her, horrified. This couldn't be happening. It just couldn't be. There had been no warning at all.

Clinging tightly to Sarah, I shook my head furiously. "Why can't I just stay here with you, Sarah? I don't want to go. Please don't make me go!"

She knelt down next to me until she was at my height. She did that when she was talking to Matthew if he did something wrong, or when she was teaching him a lesson about something. I didn't want to learn a lesson. I just wanted to stay where I was.

"I'm so sorry, Bella. If they'd let me keep you, I would. But you can visit anytime you want."

"That might not be possible," Mrs. Williams interrupted.

"What are you talking about?" Sarah asked, whirling around, her eyebrows mashed together. I rarely saw her upset, but that side of her had appeared more often since Mrs. Williams had come into our lives.

"The foster family is located on the other side of the city. It's quite a distance from here," Mrs. Williams said. "And since Bella is a minor, permission would have to be given for visits like that. In the eyes of the law, you aren't a legal guardian or a family member so it could be complicated."

"But how will I get to school each day?" I stared back at her, unable to process what was going on. I normally didn't take the bus and I wouldn't even know which one to take.

"Bella," Mrs. Williams said, rounding the couch to come closer to me.

I glared at her, already knowing what she was going to say.

"After the move, you will be attending a different school."

"What?" Sarah asked. "This transition was supposed to be easy for her. She just lost her parents, and now you want to uproot her from her school as well?"

Mrs. Williams nodded as if this wasn't a big deal. "When the transition comes all at once, it is difficult. But Bella is a smart girl. I think she will adjust well."

"Can't I take a bus or something?" I pleaded.

"It's not possible to stay at your current school," Mrs. Williams said a little more firmly. "The paperwork is already underway."

I realized that was why we hadn't heard from her in a few days. She'd planned all of this and then decided to spring it on me all at once. I was sure she hadn't expected a fight from me. Well, I didn't care. She was going to get one!

"I'm not going!" I shouted at her and ran off toward Mia's bedroom.

Slamming the door loud enough that the pictures on the wall shook, I leaned against the door, blocking her from entering. My insides twisted and I could barely breathe through the tightness in my throat.

I sank down onto the floor. Burying my head in my hands, I sobbed. I hadn't cried so much since the funeral. First, I'd lost my parents, and now some woman was telling me I had to live with strangers and I had to change schools as well. What about all my friends? What about my best friend, Abbie? Would I ever see her again?

Since the apartment was so small, Mrs. Williams and Sarah's voices carried from the other room. I couldn't hear exactly what they were saying, but I jumped up when the front door closed.

I ran to the window and waited until Mrs. Williams left the building and headed towards her car. So I wasn't going today. Maybe Sarah had convinced her to let me stay after all.

There was a knock on the door, and I turned to see Sarah's head peeking through the opening. "Can I come in?"

"Yes," I said, wiping at my face. "I saw her leave. Did you tell her she has to let me stay?"

Sarah let out a huge breath and stared at the floor.

Mia shuffled into the room behind her. She raced over to me and wrapped her little arms around my legs. "I don't want you to go, Bella. Please, can you stay with us?"

Her sad face made my heart break.

Sarah sat down on my bed; it was a spare bed that she used for guests. It wasn't the most comfortable, but I'd sleep on it forever if it meant I could stay.

She patted the spot next to her and I sat down. Mia climbed up and sat on my lap. I hugged her against me. She didn't wriggle away as she normally did. She was only two, but even she knew there was something wrong.

The sound of cartoons from the living room floated into the bedroom. Matthew's favorite show's theme song played, and I knew he was oblivious to what was happening.

"I spoke with Mrs. Williams," Sarah said. "She's giving you until the afternoon to pack your things. She'll be back later to take you to your new home."

My heart sank. "What? No, Sarah, please don't make me go—"

Sarah sighed heavily and I could see that this was almost as hard for her as it was for me. "I asked her to give you some time to pack. She's very pushy but I insisted that she come back later. It breaks my heart, Bella but there's nothing I can do. I'm so sorry."

I buried my face into Mia's mass of thick hair, and her little body turned to face me. Her chubby fingers touched my face and then she hugged me tightly.

Sarah wrapped her arm around my shoulder and pulled us both close. "Everything is going to be alright, Little Bean."

I wasn't sure how it would ever be alright, but I knew that Sarah loved me. She was the only adult who did. No matter what happened, I knew I had her, and no amount of distance would change that.

CHAPTER FOUR

The black leather seat under me was cooler than the temperature outside, almost too cool. It felt wrong. And it also felt wrong to have Mrs. Williams sitting behind the steering wheel in the seat in front of me.

Just three weeks earlier, Mom and Dad were the ones to always drive me around. Traveling from one side of the city to the other would be a happy event as we drove across town, visiting some new place or another. Their smiling faces would turn to look at me from the front seat, as we chatted and laughed.

But instead of one of my loving parents, Mrs. Williams sat there instead.

Pressing her manicured finger over the display screen of the navigation device next to her, the directions for my "new home" spoke to her from the speakers.

Her mouth was moving, but I didn't hear much over the sound of the car's hum as it sped along the road. Perhaps I was purposely blocking her out. Although, whatever she said didn't matter. Nothing mattered anymore.

"Everything is going to be fine," she said, glancing at me through the rearview mirror. Even though her tone was light, there was pity in her eyes. I could see it easily from my spot in the back seat.

It was the same look and phrase that everyone gave me. It happened at the funeral and it had happened every day since. I'd learned to hate that pitying look as well as the reassuring words that people spoke. Neither eased my mind in the slightest.

I just wished that Mrs. Williams pitied me enough to leave me where I wanted to be instead of with strangers.

When the car slowed, I peered at the house that I'd now be living in for who knew how long.

I took in the untidy façade in disgust. It was hard to see much through the overgrown trees and garden that spilled out over the pavement. The long grass seemed to be springing up from the ground like weeds.

They probably were weeds.

How could Mrs. Williams think that this mess of a house was a good place for me?

She parked the car and jumped out. Her heels clicked over the pavement as she opened the gate at the bottom of the driveway. The fence was a dirty shade of white and chipped in many places.

She got back into the car and I noticed she was panting slightly. "Okay, here we go," she said.

I chewed on my lip as the car lurched forward, bringing me closer to the house that loomed unwelcomingly in front of me. I hoped the inside was clean but seriously doubted that.

"Bella," Mrs. Williams said.

"Yes?" I murmured.

"I know this doesn't seem like much, but the Robinsons are a top-notch foster family. They've taken in many children over the years. This has been in addition to having two kids themselves. The situation you're in is not ideal for anyone, but I think you will do well here."

I swallowed. Nothing about today was ideal.

Even though my mom was no longer alive, she'd always encouraged me to make the best of every situation. Would she want me to be okay with this or put up a fight?

My parents' smiling faces were foremost in my mind. Both of them had been the most positive people I knew. I knew that Mom would want me to at least try to deal with the situation.

I let out a big breath and nodded. "Okay."

Mrs. Williams smiled and got out of the car again.

I pulled the handle on the car door alongside me and opened it. Even though it wasn't quite Spring yet, the temperature was warm enough that I didn't need a jacket.

I didn't care about impressing the Robinsons, but I had put on one of my favorite outfits.

Mom always wanted me to show off my best side to others, especially during a first meeting.

Glancing around, I could see that the sides of the property were as messy as the front. A small fence wrapped around what looked like a garden. One that appeared not to have been used for a while. There were large clumps of grass that peeked through the wire fence instead of flowers or vegetables.

At my house, well...the house I'd grown up in, Mom had taken pride in her garden. She and I spent hours on the weekends weeding and watering the plants.

The Robinsons' garden was just an unruly mess compared to my mother's.

I wondered if the new owners of my old house would keep the garden as tidy as my mom had always kept it.

Tears filled my eyes. A few of them slipped out before I could stop them. Nothing was ever going to be the same.

Mrs. Williams patted my shoulder as I took a hesitant step forward.

In my blurry vision, the house ahead of me looked almost normal. But when I cleared my tears away, it was the same ugly place that I'd spotted from the street.

Walking along the narrow path toward the front door, my shoe caught on a clump of weeds and I tripped. Mrs. Williams grabbed me with both hands before I fell.

"Are you alright?" she asked.

No, I'm not alright! I wanted to shout at her. Couldn't she see how terrible this place was? What sort of family lived here anyway?

But instead, I whispered, "I'm fine."

A twisting sensation tightened in my stomach as we

neared the front door. Mrs. Williams stuck close to me in case I tripped again. Taking a deep breath, I tried to calm myself. But that was impossible. By the time we reached the doorway, my hands were shaking. I shoved a chunk of my dark hair over my shoulder and blinked a few times to clear out the tears that were trying to fall.

Mrs. Williams rang the doorbell and we waited for my new family to open it. My heart throbbed in my chest. I glanced at the porch ceiling. Thin clumps of paint hung from the wood like bats. I wouldn't be surprised if there were rodents all over the property. But I doubted these people cared much. Why would they want extra kids if they couldn't even care for their house? Did they expect me to mow the lawn or something? That, I would definitely refuse to do.

Mrs. Williams promise from earlier echoed in my head. While I'd previously thought this was going to be a temporary place for me to stay, she said if it all turned out okay then it would be my home for years to come.

She had meant it to reassure me, but now that I'd arrived, it wasn't reassuring at all.

What if I didn't like the Robinsons?

What if they didn't like me?

Even though I usually got along with everyone, I was an only child. At this place, I would have to live with a boy and a girl, two kids who I had never met before.

Mrs. Williams said the girl was around my age. But did that mean we'd have to share a room?

What if we didn't get along?

Mrs. Williams had tried to ease my mind with all the questions I asked her about the family, but even though she was positive about it all, I wasn't so sure.

Once again, I struggled to stifle the overwhelming need to run away, to escape to a place where I could be on my own and cry. Why did my parents have to die? It was so unfair.

We'd been such a happy family. We'd had such an amazing life together. We adored each other and had such a tight bond, one that I didn't see many of my friends share with their parents.

My family was special.

Everything had been perfect until the day of the accident. It was the day that I'd remember for the rest of my life.

It was the day that changed my world forever.

CHAPTER FIVE

The door to my new home creaked open in front of me. It reminded me of a scary movie I'd seen with Abbie a while back. I had no idea what to expect.

Did this family know how difficult this was for me? How much had Mrs. Williams told them?

A large woman stood in the doorway. She had unnaturally colored red hair that was cut to the top of her shoulders. She wore a blue sleeveless shirt with small flowers embroidered on the hem. Her jeans were stained, and her slippers had a hole in the toe.

She appeared as if she hadn't even been expecting us. She stared blankly at me for a moment, looking me up and down.

Was it too late to change all of this? Couldn't I just go back to Sarah's?

"Bella," Mrs. Williams said in a chipper voice, interrupting the awkward silence. "This is Vivian Robinson."

"You can call me Viv," Vivian said. "Please, come inside." She turned around and walked into her house.

Mrs. Williams had to give me a gentle prod to get my feet moving.

Inside, there was a long hallway with several doors on either side. It was quite dark, but I could still see the deep scratches on the hardwood floors. The thin rug that ran along the middle was frayed at the edges. I glanced at Mrs. Williams. Did she see the terrible condition of this place? How could she expect me to want to live here?

Glancing up at her, I noticed that she didn't appear to be worried at all. Maybe she needed some glasses.

The few rooms that I saw were equally untidy. There were stacks of plates on the dining room table. Books and other items were strewn all over the small study.

At the end of the hallway, Viv turned into a room and Mrs. Williams and I followed her. There was a large brown sofa with a few holes in one of the cushions where fluffy white cotton poked through.

I took in the scent of some strong chemical. It appeared that Viv had tried to clean before my arrival, but the condition of the house was still terrible. No amount of cleaner would turn this into a respectable home.

Two kids sat on the couch, watching a show on a small television that sat on a rather antique looking stand in the corner. Viv snapped her fingers at them. The girl jumped up from her seat while the boy didn't even flinch.

The girl stood and moved next to her mother, locking eyes with me. She tugged at the hem of her tight t-shirt, attempting to tuck it into the top of her leggings. But the thick rolls of her stomach held the shirt in place. She looked like a miniature version of her mom except for the color of her hair.

"Turn that TV down!" Viv frowned at her son.

I jumped, startled at her tone.

"Where are your manners?" Viv snapped. "Come and say hello to your new foster sister, Bella."

I glanced up at Mrs. Williams who didn't seem bothered by the way this woman was speaking to her kids. Did she think that behavior was okay?

My parents had never spoken like that to me. If I did something wrong, we talked about it. I just hoped Viv's snappy tone wasn't a regular thing in this house, though I had an idea it might be.

The boy sighed and scooted off the couch. He looked to be about seven or eight. He stood on the other side of Viv and rolled his eyes before staring at the floor.

Viv's mouth curled upwards into a wide smile and I wondered if that was more for Mrs. Williams than for me. There was something about her that was off. She reminded me of how Principal Fletcher treated other adults compared to the way she talked to the kids at school. She was always so pleasant with adults but could be a monster to the students.

"This is my daughter, Ellie," Viv said, placing her hands on the girl's shoulders. "And this is my son, James."

"Hi," Ellie and James said at the same time without looking at me.

I chewed on my lip and gave them a small smile.

"Can I go now?" James asked. Without waiting for permission, he scrambled back to the couch and his TV. show.

Viv laughed and waved a hand at Mrs. Williams. "These kids and their shows."

Mrs. Williams laughed along with her.

Ellie rolled her eyes and I smiled.

For a moment, I thought we'd shared an inside joke, but when she saw me looking at her, she narrowed her eyes.

Wasn't this supposed to be a warm family? I didn't get that feeling at all. Mrs. Williams had talked about them so much. Apparently, it wasn't the first time they'd had foster children stay with them. Maybe Mrs. Williams was sent to the wrong house. I thought about asking her to check the address.

"Ellie, show Bella to her room," Viv said. "I want to talk to Mrs. Williams for a moment."

Earlier that day, I wanted Mrs. Williams to leave, but at that moment, I wanted to grab hold of her hand and not allow her to leave my sight. Or better yet, demand for her to get me out of this place.

"Come on," Ellie said and headed out of the room.

Mrs. Williams smiled at me. "I'll come and check on you before I go."

Great. She really was going to leave me here.

I hurried to follow Ellie down the hallway. At the end of the hall was a set of stairs. She clobbered up them with heavy footsteps and I raced to keep up with her. The stairs creaked under me. I wondered how much longer they would take Viv and Ellie's weight. Although if the stairs withstood their weight then I wouldn't have a problem. I felt bad for thinking of them in that way. I wasn't upset with them; it was more about the situation.

"Over here!" Ellie called to me from the end of the dark hallway.

"Coming!" I said and made my way towards her.

I stood in the doorway and shivered. The walls were completely bare and painted a sickly yellow color. There were two twin beds on opposite sides of the room. A small cupboard, hardly big enough for half of my clothes, stood in the corner. There was only one desk and a chair. How was I ever going to get homework done if I had to share a desk?

Ellie pulled the long string that hung from the light attached to the middle of the ceiling. It didn't do much to light the room, and it flickered every few seconds.

Walking inside, I went straight to the window. Moving aside the flimsy sheer curtain, I looked out onto the untidy garden in the side yard. Turning to Ellie, I saw her frowning. I stared quietly back at her, not sure what to say.

"Mom lets whoever uses this room decorate it the way they want. Not that the foster kids who come here have much."

"We're not sharing this room?" I asked.

Ellie snorted. "No way. My room is much nicer than this."

She certainly wasn't making me feel any better.

"Don't worry though, you have the room to yourself," Ellie said. "For the time being anyway."

For the time being?

Ellie's words rang in my head for a moment before I asked, "What does that mean?"

She smirked. There was some food coated on the corners of her mouth that I hadn't noticed before. "Well, if we get another girl, then you'll have to share this room with her."

I shook my head.

She placed her hands firmly on her hips and stomped her foot like a six-year-old. "Because no one's sharing my room. My mom said so!"

"Another girl?" I asked, looking at the spare bed that stood across the room.

Ellie shuffled over and sat down on the bed beside me. It creaked under her weight. She adjusted herself until her legs dangled off the side. Tucking her hands under her legs she swung them back and forth. "So…you need to know the rules of the house! My room is down the hall and it's out of bounds! You're not allowed in there without my permission!"

It was her house, but I wondered if the rule applied to her entering my room as well. I was about to ask when she started speaking again.

"You can only use the bathroom for ten minutes at a time — one shower a day, that's all. Otherwise, we'll run out of hot water. And besides that, water costs a lot of money. So we don't want you wasting it. Just make sure you follow the rules. Don't be like the last girl we had living with us. She always went into my room and took my things. I'm so glad she's gone!"

Again, how could Mrs. Williams think this family was good for me? Didn't she care what the people were really like or even what condition the house was in?

Ellie's threatening tone was bad enough, but what did she mean by the last girl? Where had the other girl gone? Somewhere better? Or was it worse?

Tears burned at the corners of my eyes. I wanted to tell Ellie to leave, but I had a feeling she'd make fun of me if I cried.

She wriggled off the bed and went to the window. "That last girl was so much trouble. She was relocated."

I shook my head, not fully understanding. "What do you mean…relocated?"

Ellie whipped around and squinted her eyes at me. "*Re*-located," she said the word slowly as if I hadn't heard it before. "I thought the social worker said you were smart. You'd better understand the rules, or you'll be out of here as well."

I swallowed the lump in my throat. I wanted to say something back to her, but a bigger question popped into my mind. "How many foster kids have lived here before me?"

I looked at her fearfully, waiting for her answer.

CHAPTER SIX

Ellie blew out a breath, her lips flapped as if she were blowing a raspberry. "We've had heaps of kids living with us. My parents have been fostering for years."

I shivered, thinking of all the girls who'd lost their parents or families and had to live in this place. But if they could do it, surely I could too. At least for a little while.

"A new boy is coming too," Ellie said.

My ears perked up. Another foster kid? I wondered if he'd be nicer to me than Ellie was.

She laughed. "He'll probably be here next week. And he'll have to share my brother's room."

That was a relief. I didn't think they would put me with a boy, but I wasn't sure of anything anymore.

"James hates it when a boy moves in. He never gets along with them. I don't know who these foster kids think they are when they touch things that aren't theirs."

Has this girl ever learned to share before? I didn't care to borrow her clothes but if we were going to be "sisters" we had to share some things. At least that was how Abbie got along with her sister.

Mrs. Williams had tried to convince me that I would be happy here.

She was wrong.

This wasn't like having a brother and a sister. This was more like a prison where there were strict rules about what I could and couldn't do. And I hadn't even been in the house for more than ten minutes.

"Mom said your parents died," Ellie said suddenly.

My cheeks burned as I looked at her. I nodded my head.

"That sucks," she said. "Sometimes I wonder what it'd be like to be an orphan."

My jaw dropped.

"When I think of the kids who come to live here and then go somewhere else, I'd never want their life." She laughed to herself and rubbed her belly.

My lips trembled. How could this girl be so insensitive?

Mrs. Williams' clicking heels sounded from the hallway.

Ellie whipped around and sat down on the other bed, smiling.

She reminded me of Viv. Turning on a smile in a moments notice. I'd already realized it was an act for Mrs. Williams; making out they really were caring people when they weren't at all.

Mrs. Williams appeared in the doorway and smiled at us. "What a nice room, Bella."

I silently took in my surroundings.

"Vivian said that you could decorate it any way you like," she said. "Isn't that nice?"

"It's so nice," Ellie agreed, nodding.

I hadn't brought anything with me to decorate the room with. I thought of the posters from my old bedroom that were now in storage. I wondered if I'd be able to get them. Then I thought better of it. I wanted this arrangement to be temporary.

Mrs. Williams went to the window and peered outside.

When I glanced at Ellie, I saw her smile fade into a scowl until Mrs. Williams turned around again, and then her smile reappeared.

"This room gets a lot of sun," she said. "How fortunate that you get your own room."

"For now," Ellie said under her breath. But it appeared that I was the only one who heard her.

"It will be just like having a brother and a sister," Mrs. Williams beamed at me.

Was that her mantra or something? I was sure that some kids who didn't have siblings would love to have a brother or a sister. But not me. Not one like Ellie, anyway. I didn't know much about James but from Ellie's comment about him hating to share with the foster kids, I knew I wouldn't like him.

"Let's get your bags from the car, Bella," Mrs. Williams said. "Then I'll let you get acquainted with your new family."

My new family? The thought gave me a sick feeling in my stomach.

Ellie waggled her chubby fingers in a goodbye gesture as we left the room. She obviously didn't think that I needed my own space as much as she needed hers.

Once we got outside, I asked the questions that had formed in my head while I was with Ellie. "Ellie said foster kids come here all the time. Why are there so many? She said I might have to share my room."

Mrs. Williams sighed. "The Robinsons are a charitable family. They open their door to kids who need a roof over their head."

"She said I could only use the bathroom for ten minutes a day," I added.

"They do have a well water system so I guess they need to conserve their water usage."

Mrs. Williams didn't seem bothered at all. I wondered how she'd feel if she only had ten minutes of bathroom time to herself each day. I was sure she'd hate it as much as me.

"Ellie doesn't seem to like me," I said, desperate for Mrs. Williams to understand that this was a terrible decision.

"Having new kids in the house all the time is probably a little trying, but I'm sure you will be the best of friends in no time."

She popped the lid of the trunk and lifted out two

suitcases. I couldn't believe that almost my entire life fitted into two suitcases.

I locked eyes with her. "Please don't leave me here," I begged, on the verge of tears. "I want to stay with Sarah."

Mrs. Williams squeezed my shoulder lightly. "I know this is an adjustment, Bella. But Vivian has been taking in foster kids forever. If you need anything, just ask her. I'll be back soon to check in on you."

"When?"

"I'm not sure. But in the next couple of weeks."

Even though Mrs. Williams had always been a sign of bad news, her leaving was even worse news now.

"If you go inside, you can ask Vivian or one of the kids to help you with your bags. I have another appointment so I have to leave now." She hugged me and then got into her car.

I wiped at my nose with my arm and watched her drive away. Standing in the driveway with my bags, I felt more alone than ever. The only person I wanted to be with was across town, and without Vivian's permission, I wouldn't be able to see her or her kids again. I was on my own, and I had no idea how I was going to survive.

When I lugged my bags inside the house, Vivian was nowhere to be found.

James was still in the living room watching television, and I was sure that Ellie was in her room, not wanting anything to do with me.

Instead of looking for my foster mother or asking for help, I trekked up the stairs, dragging my bags one after the other behind me. There were a few times that I nearly fell backward from the weight, but after two trips, I made it on my own.

I smiled at the small accomplishment and headed down the dark hallway toward my room. Sounds from behind a closed door nearest to the stairwell made me think it must be the door to Ellie's room. I'd be sure to steer clear of that one. I wouldn't want to be threatened by Ellie if she thought I was taking her things.

When I reached my own room I closed the door. There wasn't a lock but I placed the heavier suitcase in front of it. If Ellie was going to barge in on me, I'd know about it.

I sat down on one of the beds, my mind weighing heavily with the burden of what surrounded me. All I wanted to do was curl up and sleep forever.

Digging into my backpack for my phone, I opened my photos app. The first picture that appeared was one from last summer when my parents and I visited the beach. We'd rented the same beach house for years. The smiling faces in the photograph had no idea what was to come.

Now, none of us was ever going back to that beach house again.

Turning my phone over so it faced down, I buried my face in the pillow and sobbed. Even though I'd cried a lot over the past three weeks, this cry was different. I soaked the pillowcase within seconds as my body shook with tears.

Sarah wasn't there to comfort me.

I was in a strange home with no one who cared about

me.

The picture from the beach burned into my brain. My parents' smiling faces filled my mind.

Why did they have to die?

CHAPTER SEVEN

At some point, I fell asleep.

It wasn't until I heard my name from some far away distance that my eyes opened and reality crashed over me. I was at the Robinsons house, and my parents were gone.

I swung my feet onto the floor, still groggy with sleep as I glanced around. Outside, the sun was setting.

The doorknob rattled, and Ellie called my name once more. "Bella! Open the door right now," her muffled voice carried into the room.

As I got up from the bed, the room tilted. I felt dizzy and disoriented and had to get my bearings before moving from my spot.

Ellie banged on the door again. "You can't lock the door! That's another rule!"

But she could tell me not to go into her room? The thought flashed through my mind as I shoved my suitcase aside. Opening the door, I came face to face with her.

She barged in and glared at the suitcase. "You can't block the door like that."

"What do you want?" I asked her. I hoped she hadn't woken me up just to go over more of her "rules".

She whipped her damp hair over her shoulder, spraying water droplets all over me. "Dinner's ready. You need to come downstairs right now."

She bumped her shoulder roughly against mine as she turned back to the hallway.

Rubbing my shoulder, I followed her.

Downstairs, the sound of clanking utensils against plates made me think that they'd already started eating. Passing the kitchen, I saw the clock on the wall read five-thirty. It was so early; I wasn't even hungry. And besides that, I couldn't stop the churning anxiety in my stomach.

James was already in his seat, reaching for the spoon that sat in a large bowl of mashed potato. Vivian came in behind us, placing a huge tray of chicken on the table, already cut into pieces. It was the largest serving of chicken I'd ever seen at one time. It reminded me of how Mom brought out the turkey for Thanksgiving.

Maybe they'd prepared a special dinner for me?

A large man, who I assumed was Mr. Robinson, sat at the other end of the table. He was on his phone and hadn't looked up at all since Ellie and I came into the room.

"Dad!" Ellie called.

Mr. Robinson looked at her and then his eyes met mine. "Oh, you must be Bella?"

I nodded.

Ellie sat next to her brother, and there were two other empty chairs. I wasn't sure where they wanted me to sit, so I remained in the doorway.

"I'm Max," Mr. Robinson said with a crooked smile.

My stomach churned again. He had the same smile as Viv did when I'd arrived. It was polite but for some reason, it didn't seem genuine.

Maybe that was just their personality.

He cleared his throat and went back to his phone call.

"Sit over there!" Ellie pointed her finger at the chair across from her.

"Stop yelling!" James said, poking his sister in the arm.

"OW!" Ellie said, clutching her arm.

Their pokes turned to smacks, and the moment I sat in the chair, Max slammed his hand on the table. "Will you two quit it? I'm on the phone!"

Ellie and James' eyes opened wide, and they sat silently staring at each other, not daring to speak.

Max finished his call and then grumbled to himself,

shoving his phone into his pocket. "Can you two be civilized for once!"

Viv didn't seem to notice the tension in the room as she filled everyone's plates.

She served me last. Huge mounds of mashed potatoes and what looked like squash took up most of my plate. The chicken was piled on top.

I glanced at Ellie and James who had already eaten a large portion of their meal.

When Viv finally sat down next to me, she said, "You'd better eat up so you can head to bed and get some rest ready for your first day of school tomorrow."

"Tomorrow?" I asked.

She shoved a piece of chicken into her mouth and spoke while she chewed. "Well, you can't stay at home!"

"Do I have to go to a new school?" I asked. "I'd really like to keep going to my old school."

She shook her head. "That's not possible. It's too far away. I don't have time to drive across the city twice a day to get you there and back."

"What about the bus? I'm sure I can find one—"

"No, it's too far. It won't work," she said firmly. "You'll be fine. You'll make new friends. And you'll have Ellie to look after you. Won't she, Ellie?"

Ellie rolled her eyes and sighed, saying nothing.

Viv frowned. "It'll be fine."

Reaching across the table, Viv piled more potatoes onto everyone's plate.

When she came to me, she stopped, noticing that I hadn't touched anything yet. "What's the problem?"

Four sets of eyes were on me, and everyone stopped eating.

"I'm not very hungry," I said softly. By the way my stomach had tightened, I wasn't sure if I'd ever be hungry again.

"You have to eat!" Max said in a demanding tone. His

lips were twisted in a grimace as if not eating was the worst thing ever.

Actually, losing your parents and having to stay with a strange family was the worst.

"I'm not—"

"Eat!" he said through gritted teeth.

I shivered at his tone. No one had ever spoken to me like that, but I knew immediately that I had to obey.

I picked up my fork and stabbed at a small piece of chicken before shoving it into my mouth. It was dry and I could barely chew it. I swallowed some water from my glass to help it go down.

Everyone went back to eating while Viv asked Max about his day at work.

With them distracted, I moved my food around on my plate without taking too many more bites. The food I'd already eaten was making me feel ill.

After everyone had finished their second helpings, Viv started to collect the plates from the table. "Bella, you can use the bathroom now and get ready for bed. I left you a towel in the cupboard."

"Isn't she helping with the dishes?" Ellie whined.

Viv sighed. "It's her first night. I'll give her a pass this time."

She winked at me as if she had done me a favor.

She had, but I didn't want to let her know it.

"You'll have to help tomorrow, though," Ellie frowned at me.

I raced out of the room and into the hallway.

"Make it a quick one, or you'll use all the hot water!" Max called out loudly.

What was with all the yelling? Everyone seemed cranky all the time.

I grabbed my bathrobe from my room before entering the bathroom where I nearly slipped on something wet. Grabbing onto the door handle, I steadied myself. When I flipped on the light, I noticed the whole floor was covered with water. Even the small mat near the sink squished when I stepped on it. In the corner by the tub, a heap of wet towels was shoved against the wall. I guessed that Ellie and James had left them there.

Opening the cupboard, I found a towel for me. It was the only one in there. I tried to find a dry spot to walk, but the bottom of my jeans was already soaked. So much for not wasting water.

I thought of my bathroom at home...the home where I grew up. It adjoined my bedroom and Mom and Dad had remodeled it for my birthday. They'd allowed me to help choose all the fittings and when it was finished, I felt as if I'd walked through the pages of an interior design magazine.

Mom had bought me a set of fluffy towels that were so soft and lovely against my skin. I could picture them clearly in my mind.

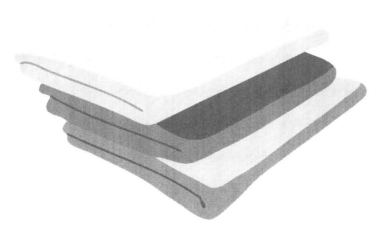

But the towel Viv had left for me was thin and scratchy. It certainly wasn't what I was used to. Trying to protect it from the water that was everywhere, I shoved it onto the rack behind the door along with my bathrobe.

I couldn't help but be reminded of how different this place was from my own home, the home that I'd lived in since I was born; the home that was no longer mine since Mrs. Williams said it was in the process of being sold. I'd never use my new bathroom again. Someone else would enjoy it instead. They'd sleep in my room and have meals in my kitchen and dining room. They'd create new memories in the place that I had treasured for so long.

My insides churned. I closed the door and locked it. Bowing my head, I couldn't help the tears that flowed down my cheeks, splashing onto the already soaked floor.

Nothing was ever going to be the same. I'd probably be stuck in this horrible place until I was old enough to move out and live on my own.

That thought made me cry even harder.

CHAPTER EIGHT

After I showered, I quickly dressed in my robe, grabbed my clothes and ran back to my room, leaving the mess behind for someone else to clean. I wasn't their maid. Although I hoped I wouldn't be blamed for it.

I had visions of Max telling me that from now on I'd only be allowed five minutes in the shower because he thought I was wasting water; when it was his own children who had splashed water everywhere.

After dressing in my pajamas, I hung my towel on the knob of my door to dry. Suddenly the door whipped open. I jumped back, barely getting out of the way as my back slammed against the cupboard. "Oww—"

Ellie burst into my room.

"Haven't you heard of knocking?" I asked.

She shrugged and went over to the spare bed. "This is my house."

I gritted my teeth and sat down on my own bed. Picking up my phone, I checked my messages, hoping that Ellie would get the hint to leave me alone.

I opened and closed a few apps before I realized she was still sitting there watching me.

"Is there something you want?" I asked, looking up to face her.

Her eyes were on my iPad. I'd left it on the bedside table and she couldn't take her eyes off it.

After a moment, she replied, "I'm bored."

She then stood up from the bed and walked over to my suitcases which I hadn't yet unpacked. I watched as she knelt down next to my things. My first impulse was to rush over and push her away. If I was going to live in her house with her bursting in whenever she wanted, I needed to be able to keep at least some things private.

I imagined her shoving her crusty mashed potato stained fingers into my neatly folded clothes. I cringed. "I'm going to bed," I said, wanting her out of my suitcases and out of my room.

She stood up and glanced at my phone. Frowning, she asked, "You have an iPhone?"

I held it close to my chest as she came closer to me. "It's an old model. It was my dad's. He gave it to me when he upgraded to a newer one."

"Your own cell phone…you must be rich!"

I glared at her as she sat down on my bed. She lifted her feet up onto the bed and sat crossed legged.

For some reason, I thought of Sarah's daughter, Mia. I'd shared her bedroom for the past few weeks and I was sure she could easily teach Ellie a few lessons on manners and respecting other people's privacy.

Thinking of Mia made me want to call Sarah, but I no longer had credit on my phone.

"Do you have Wi-Fi?" I asked.

"Maybe," Ellie said with a smirk. "Why? Do you want to chat with your *boooyfriend*?"

I rolled my eyes. Even if I did have a boyfriend, I'd never be able to see him again now that I had to go to a different school. "No. I want to call my mom's best friend, Sarah. She's the one I've been staying with. I promised to call her tonight."

The last part was a lie, but I desperately wanted to talk to Sarah. If I called her on Skype, I could see Mia's smiling face. That would cheer me up and help make staying in this strange house just a little bit easier.

Ellie glanced at my iPad again and then stretched her legs out. She leaned casually back as if she were hanging out in her best friend's bedroom. "How about I give you our Wi-Fi password and you let me use your iPad?"

"That's fine," I said without a second thought.

I turned on the internet screen on my phone and the pop up for the Wi-Fi password came up.

"The name is Robinson4," she said.

I found the name right away. It had all the bars full. That was good news.

"Password is froggie2."

I didn't bother to ask where that password came from. But after typing it in, the little check mark next to the Wi-Fi name made my heart leap.

Ellie snatched up the iPad and laid back on my bed again.

I added the Wi-Fi to my phone and opened the Skype app. Butterflies fluttered excitedly in my stomach at the thought of having internet access and being able to talk to the people who cared about me.

During dinner, I'd planned to ask about using the internet, but I hadn't dared mention it. My parents always had strict rules about internet use but I had no idea what the Robinsons' rules were. I had a feeling they must also be strict since Ellie was acting as though she were getting away with something she shouldn't.

I watched her grin widen as she downloaded a free gaming app onto my iPad. She wouldn't be able to purchase anything but I almost wanted her to try. I'd love to see the disappointment on her face when she failed.

Now that I could call Sarah though, I wanted to do it right away. I'd also promised to contact Abbie as soon as I was settled in. I couldn't wait to tell her about this place and the crazy family I was living with. But I couldn't do that with Ellie in the room.

From the corner of my eye, I watched her, sitting contentedly on my bed, her attention focused solely on the iPad. I realized it was the answer to getting her to leave. "You can take it to your room if you want."

She tore her eyes from the screen and smiled at me.

Inside, I smiled as well.

I had managed to get rid of her.

It was one victory for me.

CHAPTER NINE

Ellie jumped up from my bed and raced out of the room, leaving the door wide open. As I walked over to close it, I heard her bedroom door slam shut behind her. At least I knew how to get her out of my room from now on.

Just as I was closing my door, James suddenly appeared in front of me.
I jumped back, startled. His expression was unreadable. He wasn't smiling or frowning either. He stared at me wide-eyed.

What was with these kids and barging in on my personal space? I bet if I ever did it to them, I'd be shipped out of this house the very next day. Though, it wasn't a bad idea. If I ever got sick of them, maybe I could break one of their rules and Mrs. Williams would have to send me back to Sarah's. On the other hand, I might see the angry side of Max again, and I never wanted to see that if I could help it.

Without a word, James turned around and walked into his bedroom across the hall from mine. He closed the door, leaving me more confused than ever.

Shutting my own door. I shoved my open suitcase in front of it so I could have some privacy. I doubted Ellie would bother me again tonight and James didn't seem like he wanted to talk to me. Maybe he expected me to have another iPad or something. I had no idea really, but I was certainly not giving him my phone.

Opening the Skype app again, I dialed Sarah first. I knew it was almost Mia and Matthew's bedtime so I needed to call straight away. When Sarah's face filled the screen, a wave of emotion filled me. Tears dripped from my eyes as she and the kids waved to me from the screen.

"Bella, honey, is everything okay?" Sarah asked.

She walked into the living room and sat down on the couch. All I wanted was to be sitting next to her.

"Yes," I nodded. If I told her I was upset, it might make her feel bad and I didn't want to do that. It wasn't her fault I couldn't stay at her house. "I'm just so happy to see you," I forced my mouth into a smile.

Her eyes narrowed slightly. It was the same expression my mom always had when she suspected I was hiding something.

"I'm happy to see you too."

"I have my own room," I said, turning the camera around. I wiped at my cheeks to hide the tears as I moved the camera around the room.

"There's another bed," she said. "Are you sharing

51

with their daughter?"

I turned the phone back to my face. "No. She has a separate room down the hall."

I didn't go into detail about the possibility of having to share a room. Sarah would know I'd hate to share with a stranger, and once again, I didn't want her to feel bad.

"How are the Robinsons?" she asked. "Are they nice?"

"Yeah."

"Bella," Sarah said. "tell me what's really going on."

"They're not bad," I said, biting back what I really wanted to say about them. "It's a lot to get used to, that's all."

She nodded. "I understand. It's going to be hard for you for a while. But you can call or text whenever you need to. Night or day, okay?"

"Okay. I will."

She pressed her lips together. "I miss you, Little Bean."

"I miss you too, Sarah."

Mia whined from alongside her.

"I'm sorry, Bella," Sarah said. "But I have to get the kids to bed."

I wanted to keep her on the phone for the rest of the night. Talking to her made me feel a little less lonely and less worried about staying in a house full of strangers. But I knew it was getting late and she really had to go.

"Love you," she said and waved to me. "Let's talk tomorrow night."

"Okay. Love you too," I said as the screen went black.

I let a few more tears slip since she wasn't looking at me anymore. Teary-eyed I glanced down at my phone and thought about calling Abbie. If I skyped her she'd know I was miserable. So instead, I went to Instagram and opened up our DM's.

She'd already sent me several photos. She was always

taking pictures of the cafeteria food and writing funny messages on them. There was even a photo that Abbie had sneaked of our library teacher, Miss Wolfenhausen. Abbie had also added a phrase that Miss W. repeated constantly. I smiled at the memory of her nasal tone as she scolded all the noisy students.

SSSSHHHHH!
NO TALKING IN THE LIBRARY!!

Abbie's photos were followed by a string of texts about how much she missed me.

My smile instantly disappeared as I typed, *Miss U* into the text box.

She replied right away. *Miss U 2!!!! Tell me everything.*

I gave her the minute by minute rundown of my day, my fingers flying over the keypad as I texted, not holding back at all about the Robinsons. It was easier to type it all instead of talking about it. And at least that way, I didn't have to worry about Ellie or Viv eavesdropping and finding out what I thought about them.

That sounds TERRIBLE! Abbie typed back.

It is!

I don't want to talk about it anymore. Tell me about school I prompted her.

Abbie and I texted back and forth for some time. She made me laugh with some of her comments. I wondered if I would ever find a friend like her at my new school.

When I asked her this, she said…

Not someone as fab as me, but you'll make friends 4 sure!

"Not so sure… I replied.

We R BFFs 4EVA!! But UR so amazing. You'll fit in right away!

Not wanting to think about school the next day, I chatted with her for some time about other things she'd been up to before my eyelids became heavy. We said goodnight and I promised to message her the following afternoon. At least that would be something to look forward to.

Getting up from the bed, I reached for the string attached to the overhead lightbulb and pulled it, shrouding the room in darkness. I hopped into bed and lay awake for some time, brushing the tears that spilled from my eyes as I thought about what the following day might bring.

CHAPTER TEN

The next morning, I woke up to an early alarm that I'd set on my phone, wanting to make sure I had enough time to get ready. Sneaking down the hallway, I found the house silent. The effect was a little eerie, and goosebumps raced up my arms as I navigated the darkened space. I hadn't paid much attention before, but even if there were lights, I wouldn't turn them on for fear of waking anyone.

Entering the bathroom, I closed the door behind me and switched on the light before tiptoeing over the tiles that were still very wet. I noticed the pile of sodden towels was still in the spot by the tub where they'd been left.

I brushed my teeth and then ran a comb through my hair before deciding on a sparkly headband and sliding it into place.

In certain situations, I liked to hide behind my hair. It was almost like having a security blanket. But at a new school, I only had one chance to make a first impression. If there wasn't anything I could do about this situation, then I had to do as my mom always encouraged and try to make the best of it. When I thought I looked presentable, I sneaked back into my room and closed the door.

I wasn't sure what time everyone got up in the mornings, but I wanted to be ready for them. I checked my outfit several times. The room didn't have a mirror, but I took enough selfies, leaning my phone against a pillow, to make sure I looked okay.

Then I sat down on the bed and wondered if Ellie's friends would like me.

Ellie was much nicer after I gave her my iPad, but if she didn't want to use it anymore, then I didn't know what I could do to get her on my side.

Almost a half-hour later, after checking all my friend's Instagram updates, a knock sounded on the bedroom door.

I jumped up and raced over to it. Viv was on the other side. She wore a purple bathrobe and thick glasses.

She blinked a few times in surprise. "You're ready?"

"Yes," I said with a smile. "I wasn't sure what time we left for school."

"Not for another hour," she grumbled. "Go eat something."

I opened my mouth to ask if she was cooking breakfast as my parents and Sarah always did, but I thought better of it. She needed time to get ready too, and I didn't want to be a bother.

Following Viv out into the hallway, I saw her knock on James' door and then Ellie's, telling them it was time to get up. She then disappeared back into her own room.

At least I was ready before everyone else and didn't have to fight for the bathroom. I decided that it would be worth getting up earlier each morning just so I could use the bathroom first.

In the kitchen, I looked through the cabinets, only finding sugary cereal. A loaf of white bread sat near the refrigerator, and I wrinkled my nose. My parents had allowed me to eat what I wanted, but they were more health-conscious people. They only ever bought rye or whole grain bread. In this house though, I obviously didn't have many options. So I decided on one of the sugary cereals.

Sitting on the couch in the living room, I turned on the television and watched the program that appeared on the screen. By the time the others came downstairs, I was finished eating.

"Why is the T.V. on?" James asked, peeking into the room.

I looked at him and shrugged. "I turned it on."

"I'm telling Ma!" he yelled as he raced from the room.

I wasn't sure what to think. He'd been in front of the television all afternoon the day before. Was watching television in the mornings not allowed? Shaking my head in confusion, I turned back to the screen and watched the weather report.

There was no word from Viv until it was time to leave. She came into the room — still in her bathrobe — and grabbed the remote from next to me, shoving her thumb into the POWER button. "Put your dishes in the sink and let's go."

"Okay," I said, slinking by her.

Ellie and James were in the hallway smirking at me. I wasn't sure what the joke was, but I decided to ignore them.

"Goodbye kids," Viv said when I returned to the hallway. "Have a good day at school." She kissed the tops of James and Ellie's heads and shooed us out the door.

Once we were outside, I asked Ellie, "Are we taking the bus?"

"No," she said. "We walk to school."

"What do you when it rains?" I asked.

"Then we bring an umbrella," she said. I noticed a silent *duh* at the end of her sentence.

It was yet another change from my old life that I'd have to get used to. I couldn't imagine that Viv would allow her kids to walk to school in the snow, but I guessed I'd have to wait and see. Or maybe by the time it snowed again, I would be back with Sarah. I would never give up hope on that, and reminded myself to focus on being able to leave at some stage so I could go back to my old school.

I followed along behind Ellie and James, noticing that the pavement wasn't wide enough for them to walk side by side. With each step, they fought over who walked on the sidewalk or the grass. I stayed a few steps behind them, watching them shove each other. A few times, I thought Ellie was going to fall on her butt. James was strong for such a young kid and he was a big boy, just like his father.

Eventually, Ellie let out a groan and stopped walking. She waited for me and I had to move onto the grass to give her room on the concrete.

She raised her eyebrows at me. "You look nervous."

I nodded. "I am nervous. It's a new school."

She shrugged. "It's not a big deal. It's just school."

"I guess," I said.

"Did you have a lot of friends at your old school?" she asked.

"Kind of. But I mostly spent time with my best friend, Abbie."

"I bet you had a lot of friends wearing those clothes," she said as if she hadn't heard me.

I looked down at what I was wearing. I'd chosen a white pleated skirt with a red knitted top and converse sneakers. It wasn't overly showy, so what was she talking about?

"Your shoes are so white," she said.

"They're leather so it's easier to keep them clean," I replied. "My mom gave them to me for my birthday. I love them so much."

"You *are* rich," she said.

I looked at her. She was being serious. It was the same comment from the night before when she'd asked about my phone.

"My parents said you came from a rich part of town. So if you lived there, your parents must have had plenty of money."

"I don't know," I shook my head, wishing she'd stop talking about my parents and money. I wasn't comfortable with what she was saying at all. My parents both worked hard and even though Dad was a top executive in the city, we definitely weren't the wealthiest family at my old school.

"My parents said you'll probably get a big inheritance one day. Is that true?"

"I don't know," I repeated, which was partly true.

Mrs. Williams had said it would take some time for the estate to be settled. But anything that my parents left for me would be mine when I turned eighteen. I wasn't sure what that would involve, but Mrs. Williams said she'd keep me updated. It wasn't something I thought about. I'd rather have my parents alive than their money any day.

Ellie kept prattling on, asking me questions about the things I owned and the vacations I'd been on, which gave her more reasons to think I had a lot of money. Asking personal questions didn't seem to bother her at all. But I wanted to keep the peace with her so I answered her as best I could.

A few minutes later, the school appeared in front of us. James and Ellie groaned at the same time. Their steps slowed as if they were walking through thick mud. As much as they didn't want to go to school, and I felt anxious myself, I was also a little excited.

Ellie's questions stopped once we walked onto the property. I took in the kids milling around on the front lawn of the long one-story building. The gray brick was clean—unlike the Robinsons' house—and the lawn was nicely manicured.

I tried to distract myself by looking at the art projects on the windows of the first floor, but I was aware of all the eyes on me as we walked into the building. Everyone seemed to be staring.

Nervous butterflies fluttered madly in my stomach. This was much more nerve-wracking than I thought it would be.

I took a deep breath, as I scanned the hallways ahead of me.

CHAPTER ELEVEN

Once we were inside, Ellie nudged my shoulder. "It's always like this when there's a new kid at school."

"Like what?" I asked, pretending not to notice everyone looking at me. I didn't want to make a big deal of all the attention I was getting. For some reason, I figured she wouldn't like that.

A little smile crossed her face, and I knew it had been the right thing to say.

James went down a different hallway, but Ellie and I kept walking down the main one. The floors were shiny and clean reflecting the lights above us. The lockers were the school colors: maroon and gold. It was a nice touch, and it made me feel better that this school had some pride in its presentation at least, and wasn't some rundown dump that I would have to face every day.

At the end of the hallway, there was another door leading outside.

"Shouldn't I go to the front office?" I asked.

"No," Ellie said. "We're in all the same classes."

"How do you know that?"

"Because that's how it works. Mom made sure of that so I could take you around and make it easier."

I didn't question it, but I still was a little suspicious of her being so nice to me. Maybe the iPad trick was enough for her to like me, after all.

Outside, there was a little courtyard. There weren't as many kids out there but I certainly caught their attention.

Again, I tried to ignore it.

Ellie moved quickly toward a girl who was waiting for her and sat down alongside her. The girl stared at me.

She had dark brown eyes and long dark hair. Her cheeks were round like Ellie's, but she wasn't nearly as overweight.

"This is Sophie Watson," Ellie said. "She's my best friend."

"Hi, Sophie," I said.

Sophie smiled and looked me up and down. "I like your shoes."

"Thanks," I said.

Sophie looked at Ellie then back to me. "You must have a lot of money."

I sighed. What was this obsession with money?

"They were a present," I said.

"From her *mom*," Ellie said to Sophie.

I frowned and looked around the courtyard. All the unfamiliar faces made my insides twist into tight knots. I wanted to get away from the conversation about my parents and their money, but I had nowhere else to go.

"How much was your skirt?" Sophie asked. "I bet it's dry-clean only."

I wasn't sure what that meant or why they cared so much. I was about to say something to get them off the subject, but the bell rang.

Ellie and Sophie stood up at the same time and slung their bags over their shoulders. "We should go."

I followed them inside, but I stayed a few steps behind them. They'd already moved on to talking about something else. I didn't care to talk about my clothes anymore so I hoped they'd forget I was behind them.

Instead, I tried to memorize the hallways. I found two sets of bathrooms on the way to class. If I needed a break, I could always use the hall pass and go into one of those for some privacy.

Our classroom was at the end of a long corridor, close to the front entrance of the school. If anything, I'd be able to wait in there when I arrived the following morning while Ellie met up with Sophie. Maybe I could make up some excuse, that way I wouldn't have to hear them talk about my clothes anymore.

Inside the classroom, there were already a bunch of kids standing around or sitting at their desks. A few of them turned my way as Ellie took me over to the teacher.

"This is Bella Barlow," Ellie said and then turned, leaving me alone at the front of the room.

"Hi, Bella," the teacher said. She was a small brown-haired woman with a kind smile and very straight teeth. "I'm Miss Harmon." Her voice was kind of high-pitched, but she seemed nice.

She put her hands on my shoulders and turned me around to face the others.

"Class, I'd like your attention please," she said.

My cheeks almost burst into flames as everyone in the classroom, except for Ellie and Sophie who were giggling together in the middle of the room, turned to face me.

"This is Bella Barlow," Miss Harmon said.

I tried to take in all the faces, but my eyes blurred.

Bella, don't you dare cry, I repeated in my mind over and over.

"Let's all make Bella feel welcome and say hello."

"Hello, Bella," the class chorused in a monotone voice. It reminded me of when I met James and Ellie and it was as though someone had to force the niceness out of them.

"You can sit in the third row, over there," Miss Harmon said to me, pointing at an empty seat. It wasn't anywhere near Ellie, and that was a relief. At least I could get a break from her during the school day. She didn't seem broken up about it either.

During attendance, I tried to match the names to faces as Miss Harmon called out each name. But halfway through roll call, my mind wandered back to my old school. My teacher, Mrs. Evans, had stopped calling out attendance earlier in the year. She already knew our faces and checked our names off her list just by scanning the room. It gave us a little more social time in the mornings. Abbie and I always chatted until the last possible second before we had to start class.

I pictured all the familiar faces in my old class. There was no need for me to worry about what others thought of my clothes or how much my parents made. Today though, things were very different.

My heart skipped a beat as I remembered my old class was going on a trip to the city science center that day. Abbie hadn't mentioned it when we were chatting the night before. Maybe that was intentional because she knew how disappointed I'd be to miss it. I remembered the day Miss Evans had first mentioned it. She even set up a countdown calendar at the back of the room. It was all everyone could talk about.

I wondered if Abbie got her wish and was assigned to be in Will Blackstone's group the way she'd hoped. She had a huge crush on Will, and I imagined she'd be smiling the whole day if she and Will were placed together. She'd probably try to sneak some photos of the two of them. I just hoped she'd finally have the courage to talk to him, something that I'd been pushing her to do for ages.

A loud *clap* broke through my thoughts, and I jolted back to the present.

Miss Harmon and half the class was staring at me. Her smile was gone, and her hands were clasped together as if she had just clapped them loudly. That must have been the sound I'd heard.

"Bella," Miss Harmon said. "Are you listening?"

"Y-yes," I stammered and glanced at the rest of my classmates.

Ellie and Sophie both stared at me as well.

"Then what is the answer?" Miss Harmon asked.

My face heated up and I knew my cheeks were redder than apples. I hoped she'd repeat whatever question she had asked, but I had no such luck. She stood there with her arms crossed and the toe of her shoe tapping against the floor.

She sighed and said, "Which kind of verb does not take an object?"

How long had I been in my head for? Everyone had their English books open while my desk was still empty. The silence stretched on, and Miss Harmon's eyebrows climbed up her forehead with each passing second.

"I-I don't know," I said, hoping she would move on.

She did, but not before instructing me to get my book open and pay attention.

I glanced at Ellie and she smirked at me.

It was obvious she wasn't on my side.

And I knew that no one else was either.

CHAPTER TWELVE

Miss Harmon didn't call on me for the remainder of the morning lessons. I knew I probably hadn't made a very good first impression and I was glad when the bell finally rang for recess.

Since my desk was situated towards the side of the room against the windows, I was one of the last kids out the door. I had no idea where recess was held, but when I looked for Ellie, she'd already raced off ahead of me with Sophie by her side.

I peered over the heads of my classmates and the other kids rushing down the hallway, but I lost sight of Ellie in the crowd before I could catch up with her.

I'd never seen her move so quickly and I had a feeling she'd rushed off on purpose in the hope of avoiding me. So much for showing me around the school the way Viv had promised.

In the hope that everyone went to the same place for recess, I thought about just following the crowd. But I wasn't sure if that was the right thing to do. My chest tightened, and I found it hard to breathe. I debated on going back into the classroom to ask Miss Harmon, but I didn't want her to get annoyed with me again.

I was just about to turn back when I felt someone tap on my shoulder. Whipping around anxiously, I found myself face to face with a very pretty brown-haired girl smiling at me.

"Hi," she said. "I'm Olivia."

"Hi," I replied shyly. "I'm Bella."

She smiled again. "Yeah, I know. Everyone's talking about you because you're new. Do you want to hang out with my friends and me?"

I swallowed, unsure if she was being genuine. After the way Ellie behaved, I wasn't really sure what to expect from the other kids at this school. But Olivia certainly seemed friendly enough.

"Come on," she said, looping her arm with mine.

By the time we reached the courtyard, I'd relaxed a little. Olivia pointed out a few things along the way, such as which bathrooms were the best to use and where to sit at lunch. She really did seem genuinely nice, but when we walked toward her group of friends sitting together on some bench seats, my heart skittered again.

There were at least eight kids all staring at me. I gulped nervously as I approached them, uncertain as to how they would react to someone new joining their group.

"Hey, guys," Olivia said. "This is Bella. The new girl."

"You live with Ellie Robinson?" a blond girl immediately asked.

"Yeah, I do," I said.

The girl nodded but didn't comment.

Someone else asked, "Are you staying with her for long?"

I barely opened my mouth before a boy spoke up, "You don't look like the regular foster kids who stay at her place."

"Um, thanks…I think?" I wasn't sure if that was meant to be a compliment or not, but they all laughed. "I'm not sure how long I'm staying," I added quickly.

Olivia and her friends were friendly but very curious; although I couldn't hold that against them. I would have been curious too. Especially since the Robinsons were always fostering kids.

"Where did you get your skirt?" Olivia asked. "It's so pretty!"

"Thanks," I said. "Um…I got it from a store when I was on vacation with my parents."

"Ooohh, where was that?" she asked.

I knew exactly where it came from, but I wasn't sure what they'd think if I told them I'd bought it at a boutique store in California. I didn't want them all thinking I was rich the way that Ellie and Sophie did.

But before I could reply another girl stepped up next

to me. "I like your shoes," she smiled as she glanced down at my feet.

I looked at my shoes and then at the pair she was wearing. I could see that hers were the same brand except in black. Hers were a little more worn, but it was clear we had something in common.

She smiled back at me. "Your white ones are much nicer than mine. But how do you keep them so clean?"

"She's obsessed with converse!" Olivia grinned.

When no one mentioned the price of my clothes and didn't make any comments about money, I started to relax. They weren't making me feel uncomfortable because of a few nice clothes that I owned.

"Did your parents really die in a car crash?" a boy sitting next to Olivia suddenly asked.

An uncomfortable silence clouded the group as everyone turned to stare at him.

He stared blankly back at them. "What? That's what everyone's saying. I'm just asking her if it's true."

"You're unbelievable!" Olivia frowned. "You never think before you speak."

Even though she and the other kids seemed annoyed with him, I could see they were all still waiting for my answer. But the question had startled me. No one had ever asked me outright before.

I tried to swallow the lump in my throat but found it very difficult. I didn't trust my voice and I certainly didn't want to start crying in front of them all. So, I didn't dare utter a word. Instead, I gave a small nod.

Olivia frowned and touched my arm. Everyone in the group remained silent, unsure what to do or say. It was very awkward and uncomfortable. And even though I wasn't the one to ask the question, I felt responsible for making everyone feel bad.

I blinked several times, praying for the tears that threatened at the corners of my eyes to stay away.

CHAPTER THIRTEEN

For the rest of the day, I followed Olivia and her friends between classes. While they seemed willing to include me, after the awkward conversation about my parents, I no longer felt relaxed around them. But it was better than being on my own.

During lunch, the girls were only interested in talking about the latest clothes they'd bought. And they spent the entire break chatting about some new store in town and the things they were planning to buy.

A few of them wore makeup and they soon moved onto that topic. But I had very little to say. Even though my parents had bought me clothes whenever I needed them, clothes weren't something I obsessed over like these girls were doing. And I hadn't been allowed to wear make-up. Obviously, the rules at this school were very different to my old one because Mrs. Fletcher had even banned nail polish. I knew she'd have a fit if she saw the variety of lip gloss several of these girls were wearing.

I tried to join in the conversation when I could, but I didn't really have much to say, and they were happy enough to talk amongst themselves.

I reminded myself to be grateful that Olivia had invited me into her group, especially as Ellie had run off and left me on my own. Even if I didn't have a huge amount in common with these girls, they didn't seem to gossip or talk meanly about other kids, and I felt a lot better about hanging out with them than with Ellie and Sophie.

Even so, I missed my old school and Abbie and all my other friends more than ever. I was an outsider in this place, and I didn't like it at all.

After school, I made sure to keep up with Ellie so she didn't abandon me again. My main concern was that I'd be able to find my way back to her house. That morning, we'd turned down a few different streets and I wasn't completely sure of the route to take.

Spotting Ellie already on the sidewalk in front of the school, I ran to catch up to her. With my bag filled with new textbooks and no time to get to my locker after school, I was out of breath when I reached her. "Ellie, wait."

She stopped in her tracks and narrowed her eyes at me. "Did you have fun with your new friends?" She flipped her hair over her shoulder, as if to mimic me.

I never flipped my hair like that, but I knew what she was doing.

"I wouldn't have had to make new friends if you didn't run off and leave me behind at recess."

"I didn't run off," she said. The tops of her cheeks turned a light shade of pink. She knew she was caught out but she continued on regardless. "You know they only like you because you've got nice clothes and the latest converse shoes. And because you're pretty!"

Before I could say anything else, she stormed off in front of me.

I already had the idea that she was jealous of me when she came into my room and saw my iPad and phone, but her blowing up at me now was mean and horrible. The only reason I was living with her was because my parents had died. Didn't she understand how hard all of this was for me?

I remained several feet behind her but made sure to keep her in my sights. I wasn't sure where James was or even if Ellie was supposed to wait for him. But that wasn't my problem. I had enough to worry about.

On the way, I took notice of houses and landmarks and the streets that we turned into so I'd know how to get to and from school on my own. I doubted it would get easier with Ellie and had a feeling I'd be walking on my own a lot from now on. But then at least that way, I wouldn't have to put up with her moods and her attitude.

When I reached the house, I found that Ellie had headed straight for the kitchen and was already stacking a pile of leftovers onto a plate. It looked to be almost as much as Viv had given us for dinner the night before.

When I caught Ellie's eye, she ignored me and headed into the living room where James was already seated in front of the television, the volume blaring loudly.

I didn't see Viv or Max anywhere, so I went up to my room. Ellie hadn't asked if I wanted something to eat but I wasn't hungry anyway. What I wanted most was time on my own, and I closed the door firmly behind me, leaning against it for a moment as I took in my surroundings.

I still hadn't unpacked properly and I had a lot of homework to catch up on. But all I wanted to do was talk to Abbie. Ignoring the clothes spilling from the open suitcase on the floor, I glanced around for my iPad. It was so much better to skype on that than the small screen on my phone. But I remembered Ellie hadn't returned it yet.

I was sure she was probably hoping I wouldn't ask for it back just yet and would most likely be annoyed if I did. So, rather than having to deal with a possible confrontation, I pulled my phone from my pocket and texted Abbie instead.

How was the field trip?

Within seconds, I heard the pinging sound of her reply.

Oh my gosh, it was so fun! But I missed U so much. Wish U could have been there!!

Me 2!! I replied, sitting on my bed.

I leaned back, laying my head on the pillow as I continued to type.

Were U in Will's group?
YES!!!!!

I grinned. *How did that go? Have U talked to him yet??*

Three little dots skittered across the bottom of the message and I knew she was typing a reply. While waiting, I imagined her and Will together…Abbie smiling and chatting and Will telling her he had a crush on her. It would be just like the scene of a movie. The smile widened on my face as I pictured the image in my head. It was so unfair that I wasn't there to witness their moment.

A knock on my door caught me by surprise and I shoved my phone under my pillow. I just hoped it wasn't Ellie asking to borrow something else.

I hopped off the bed to open the door. But before I could reach it, it swung open and I nearly bumped into Viv who was barging in, in exactly in the same way her daughter had.

"How was your day?" she asked, crossing her arms.

I took a few steps back from her. "It was okay."

"Here," she said, thrusting her hand out to me.

I looked down to see a few dollar notes in her hand. "What's that for?"

"You have a weekly allowance, so you'd better make it last. Each Tuesday will be your 'payday'."

I wasn't sure where the money had come from, but I certainly wasn't going to say no. "Thank you," I smiled at her as I took the money from her palm."

She turned around and said, "Be sure you're down for dinner on time tonight."

Since I knew what to expect, dinner wasn't as bad as on my first night. I made sure to eat so I wouldn't upset Max, and I stayed silent, allowing Ellie and James to be the focus of the meal.

When Viv asked me about school, I felt Ellie's eyes on me. "It was good, thanks. Ellie introduced me to Sophie. She's nice. Everyone at school is."

"Well, isn't that lovely," Viv said, preening at her daughter.

Ellie tilted her head to the side while still narrowing her eyes at me. I hoped she realized I was doing her a favor. I wondered how Viv would react if I told her what had really happened.

After dinner, I helped with the dishes then took a shower, once again in a flooded bathroom. By the time I was finished, I was exhausted and feeling drained of all energy, but I still had at least an hour's worth of homework to do. I hoped Miss Harmon wouldn't be too harsh on me if I didn't complete everything. After all, everyone else had been given a lot more time to work on the assignments. Hopefully, she'd allow me to catch up over the weekend.

I was just climbing into bed when someone knocked on my door. I knew who it was before the door burst open.

Ellie stormed in wearing a ratty pink bathrobe. "You

need to clean up the bathroom so I can use it."

"I didn't make the mess," I said. I knew James had showered before dinner and left the floor soaked again with soggy towels strewn all over the floor. "It was like that when I went in," I added, frowning.

"It doesn't matter," Ellie said, digging her hands into her hips. "You were the last one to use it, so you have to clean it up. If you don't, I'm going to tell Mom."

She turned and stomped down the hallway, slamming her bedroom door closed. All I wanted to do was go to bed. But I felt certain that an argument with Ellie would get me into trouble and would be one I couldn't win anyway. Sighing with frustration, I went into the bathroom and used my own bath towel to mop up all the water. I left the towel in the bathtub with the soaking wet ones James had used.

My cheeks were flushed with anger that I had to clean up his mess as I knocked hard on Ellie's door. The sound of her stomping footsteps made the floor vibrate as she moved towards it, abruptly whipping it open.

"Bathroom is clean," I said. "And I want my iPad back."

She blinked at me. "I don't have it."

"What do you mean?" I asked. "I let you borrow it last night."

She rolled her eyes. "Last I saw, James was using it."

She pushed past me and disappeared into the bathroom.

My heart raced. Why was she so difficult? And I couldn't believe she'd given her little brother my iPad without my permission. I wouldn't have minded lending it to James, but it would be nice to be asked first.

I went to his room and knocked on the door.

After knocking three more times, he finally opened it.

"What?" he asked, rubbing his eyes.

"Ellie said you have my iPad—"

"I don't!" he said quickly, his eyes widening.

I could tell he was lying. His gaze dropped to the floor and he could no longer look at me.

"I don't care if you used it, I just want it back."

"I don't have it!" he screamed.

I stepped back from him. "There's no need to scream. Can you please just tell me where it is."

"No!" he yelled, stomping his foot. "I told you I don't have it!"

The door to Viv and Max's bedroom opened from down the hallway.

"What's all this racket?" Max shouted. "Go to bed. All of you!" He then disappeared back into his bedroom, slamming the door behind him.

This was followed by James slamming his door as well. It flew shut right in my face. I took a small step backward and stood there, stunned.

I had no iPad, I had no idea where it was and I had no one on my side.

I stared around me in despair.

CHAPTER FOURTEEN

I was tempted to search Ellie's bedroom while she was in the shower but I didn't dare. It wasn't worth the risk of getting caught. With no other option, I went to my room and climbed into bed, but it was a long time before I was finally able to fall asleep. When I did, I tossed and turned constantly. At one point, I woke up to discover my face wet with tears and my pillow and sheets soaked in sweat.

In the morning when my alarm went off, my head was in such a fog that I knew I'd barely slept at all. Dragging myself out of bed, I headed quietly to the bathroom to splash cold water on my face and clean my teeth.

Since I knew I'd be in trouble if I took another shower, I did the best that I could to refresh myself with water from the basin. My hair was a tangled mess, and it took a while to comb out the knots before I could tie it up into a high ponytail.

I hoped that today would be a better day, but somehow I doubted that would be the case. I wondered why the Robinsons bothered with foster kids at all if they were going to treat them so terribly. If they didn't want me around, they shouldn't have signed up to take me into their home.

No one else was awake so I went downstairs and poured some cereal into a bowl. As I covered it with milk and began eating, I thought about the money that Viv had given me. I wasn't sure I could trust Ellie and James not to take it so I made a mental note to find a good hiding spot for it.

After washing up my bowl, I went into the living room to watch television.

Viv hadn't mentioned anything about it being against the rules in the mornings so I flicked through a few channels and settled myself on the couch. When I noticed something digging into my lower back, I turned around to see what it was. In the semi-darkness, I spotted the corner of an object that seemed to have been shoved beneath the cushion. When I yanked it out, all I could do was stare in horror at what was in my hand.

Blinking a few times, I gaped wide-eyed, my mind in a whirl of disbelief. I knew it was my iPad because of the two emoji stickers I'd added to the bottom of the frame ages ago. But instead of being relieved to have my iPad back, I was horrified. Although the room was dark, there was enough light from the television to see the shattered screen. Cracks sprayed out in every direction creating a wild web of destruction.

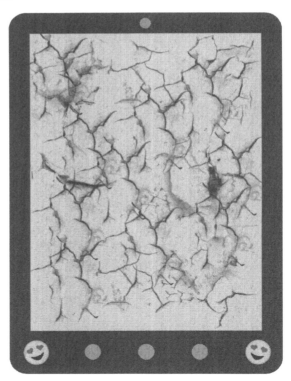

When I tried to turn it on, the screen flashed for a brief moment before it went black again. The charging icon appeared telling me the battery was drained, but even if I charged it, the screen was so badly damaged, I knew I'd never be able to use it. Tears filled my eyes. I couldn't believe that Ellie or James had broken it and then tried to hide it from me.

At the sound of their footsteps on the stairs, I darted angrily into the kitchen.

Ellie was the first to appear.

"Did you break my iPad?" I blurted, shoving it out in front of her.

She looked down at the damaged object in my hands and her eyes widened. "I didn't do that. It was fine when I gave it to James."

He appeared behind Ellie and I turned on him. "James, did you do this?"

"No!" he shrieked loudly and pushed passed me.

"What is with all the yelling this morning?" Viv complained, shuffling into the kitchen. She looked as if she'd just rolled out of bed.

"One of them broke my iPad," I said to her, holding it out for her to see.

"Kids?" Viv asked. "Did you break Bella's iPad?"

"No," James and Ellie both said at the same time.

"They were the last ones to use it," I glared at each of them and then back at Viv.

She looked at the iPad and shrugged. "If they said they didn't do it, then they didn't do it."

"But they're lying!" I struggled to resist the urge to yell at her.

"Now, now, there's no need for accusations. If you're going to have expensive things like that in the house, then they're your responsibility. You can't be blaming everyone else if something gets broken."

My lips trembled. I could not believe that Viv was

going to do nothing about this, nothing whatsoever. My eyes darted towards Ellie and James who were both staring smugly, an amused smile on each of their faces. Viv had already moved to the kettle and was filling it with water at the sink. It was obvious she didn't care at all.

I had to get away from them. I glared angrily at Ellie and James one more time then raced upstairs to my bedroom.

Throwing the useless iPad into the cupboard on top of a pile of clothes, I slammed the cupboard door shut as several tears rolled down my cheeks. Slumping down heavily onto my bed, I pushed my face into the pillow. All I wanted was to go back to Sarah's, back to my old school and my old life. More than anything, I wanted my mom and dad. How was I ever going to survive without them?

About twenty minutes passed before I heard Viv calling me from the bottom of the stairs. "You need to get down here now or you'll be late for school!"

Sighing heavily, I made my way to the kitchen. Ellie and James were finishing breakfast. I couldn't even look at them.

Viv stood up from the table to get more coffee. "You all need to get going now, or you'll be late."

Ellie and James stood up to leave, their bags were slung over their backs as they headed out the door, calling goodbye to their mother as they went.

I didn't bother to catch up with them. I knew that being anywhere near them would make me even more upset. I could see that Ellie didn't want to be near me either. For someone who was so overweight, she certainly moved fast. She was already on the sidewalk headed to school before I closed the front door.

At school, I didn't bother with her at all. As soon as the bell rang for morning recess, she and Sophie ran off but that was fine with me. I didn't want to sit with them anyway. Olivia and her friend, Maddie waited for me outside the classroom and we walked to the courtyard together.

Everyone was friendly when they saw me approach and there were no traces of the awkwardness from the day before. I did my best to join their conversation. It was a nice feeling to be included, and so different to the way I felt at the Robinsons.

At the same time though, my mind drifted to thoughts of Abbie and my other friends at my old school. As the minutes ticked by, I formed a plan in my head. I decided that as soon as I could, I would tell Mrs. Williams how bad everything was. Surely then she'd allow me to go back to Sarah's. Or, if not, perhaps I could at least move in with another foster family who lived close to Sarah and close to my old school. That would be so much better than the situation I was in now.

The thoughts floated through my mind as the kids around me chatted and laughed. Glancing aimlessly around the surrounding courtyard, my eyes fell upon Ellie and Sophie who were sitting directly opposite. Their eyes were locked on mine and I realized they'd been staring. I could feel their anger from where I sat.

Shaking my head, I turned away. I had no idea what their problem was but I hadn't done anything to them. If they were jealous that I was sitting with Olivia and the others, that was their concern, not mine.

Olivia poked me gently in the side and grimaced. "Why is she staring at you like that?"

"I don't know," I sighed. I wanted to confide in her but I didn't know her well enough. And if Ellie found out I'd been talking about her, it could cause even more trouble.

Maddie overheard us talking and rolled her eyes. "Ellie's never nice to anyone! What's it like living with her anyway? Do you even get on with her?"

Unable to help myself, I mumbled, "It's horrible. I

hate it."

"Her and her brother are so weird," Maddie added, darting a quick glance back at Ellie. "I feel so sorry for you having to live with them!"

"Hopefully it won't be for long!" I murmured quietly.

Neither Maddie nor Olivia commented but I could see the sympathy in their eyes. And that was something I disliked the most. I didn't want everyone to feel sorry for me. All I wanted was my life back.

After the morning break, I saw Ellie and Sophie heading down the hallway from the opposite direction. Before I could move out of their way, both girls separated, walking on either side of me and barging their shoulders into mine, one after another. Sophie said something under her breath which I didn't quite catch. As they continued past, all I could hear was the sound of their laughter.

Over the next few days, I tried to stay as far away from Ellie as I could. At home, we barely spoke. And except for barking orders at me to do chores, no one else said very much to me either.

Even though I hated it, I continued to clean up the bathroom after James. That way, Ellie had no reason to accuse me of making a mess, and as long as I could find a clean towel to use the following day, I was able to manage.

The less confrontation with Ellie, the better.

Meanwhile, I promised myself never to let Ellie or James borrow anything of mine again. Viv wanted me to be responsible, so it was my responsibility to keep my things away from her children.

However, this didn't stop Ellie from using use my things without my permission. When I realized my favorite nail polish was missing and saw her wearing it on her fingernails, I lost all control. "That's my nail polish. How dare you take it from my room!"

"It's my nail polish! You must have the same color!" She waved her messily painted fingers in front of me. "You're just trying to get me into trouble."

I glared angrily back at her, knowing there was nothing I could do. But when my favorite bangle, a gift Abbie had given me for my birthday went missing, there was no way I was going to let Ellie get away with that!

While she was in the shower, I sneaked into her room, praying that no one would catch me. If they did, I decided I really didn't care. I wanted my bangle back, regardless of what happened. Closing the door quietly behind me, I glanced around her messy room, thinking she'd probably hidden it somewhere. But instead, I spotted it almost immediately, sitting in plain view on her dresser.

Snatching up the bangle, I headed quickly back to the door. Just as I reached for the knob, the door swung open and I had to step back to avoid being hit.

Ellie stared back in surprise but her expression quickly turned to anger at finding me in her room. I could see she hadn't showered yet and realized she must have forgotten something. But instead of feeling guilty or intimidated, I stood my ground.

"How dare you take my things!" I held up the bangle for her to see.

Her mouth opened and closed a couple of times and she reminded me of a fish gasping for air. I didn't bother giving her a chance to defend herself or to make up some type of story. Instead, I poked her angrily in the chest as I spat the words in her face. "You dare take anything of mine ever again and I'm telling Mrs. Williams!"

Without another word, I shoved roughly past her, this time, making sure it was me who barged into her shoulder instead of the other way around.

After that, I no longer noticed anything missing from my room, although I did make every effort to hide anything valuable, including the money Viv gave me which I tucked away in a secret compartment in the bottom of my suitcase. It was the perfect hiding place and I was certain that Ellie would never find it. To be sure of that, I left a few clothes scattered on top, in case she ever did think to look inside. But the compartment was not obvious anyway. Even I hadn't realized it was there until the third time I'd used the bag.

I enjoyed the wary looks she gave me after our confrontation, although these didn't last long. It was only a matter of a day before she was back to her rude, annoying self.

During every break at school, I continued to hang out with Olivia and her friends. Even though I didn't really fit into the popular crowd, they welcomed me and this added to Ellie's annoyance.

At least this gave me a small feeling of power over her and I reveled in that fact.

It was the one positive thing I could cling to.

CHAPTER FIFTEEN

The weekend dragged on and I waited and waited for Mrs. Williams to show up. She said she'd come to check on me and I was desperate to speak to her about how unhappy I was. So far though, there had been no sign of her.

Meanwhile, Ellie and James spent almost every spare moment in front of the television. I was glad I had a heap of homework to finish as it gave me something to do as well as a chance to avoid everyone.

On Sunday afternoon, I chatted to Abbie for over an hour. Ellie barged into my room at one point. I was sure she'd probably heard my laughter and was wanting to know what I was up to. I raised my eyebrows questioningly at her and she glared back. She then left just as abruptly, slamming the door behind her.

Being able to laugh with Abbie as we chatted on skype felt so good. And I listened intently as she told me all about Will and everything that had happened over the past week. He was constantly asking to borrow her felt pens and I smiled as I imagined every scene she described.

"He obviously likes you!" I grinned.

"Maybe!" Abbie sighed then clutched dramatically at her heart as if she were in love.

"I told you all you had to do was to talk to him," I giggled back.

I wished more than ever that I could be back at my old school with my best friend. I missed her so much.

Just as I ended the call, my phone started ringing and I saw Sarah's name pop up on the Skype screen. When I clicked connect, Mia's cute little face appeared.

"Bella!" she squealed as soon as she saw me.

I was so happy to see her beautiful chubby face and I listened to her chat away about her visit to the park and how she'd fallen over and scraped her knee. She then went on to announce that she was brave and didn't cry, proudly pulling her knee into view so she could show me the scrape on her skin. She was the cutest little girl. I wanted her for my sister, instead of the mean "foster sister" I'd been forced to live with.

But the call was interrupted by the sound of Viv's voice yelling out my name. It seemed that all these people could do was yell at each other. With a sigh, I said a quick goodbye to Sarah and Mia and made my way along the hallway and down the stairs, where I could hear Viv speaking to someone in the living room.

My heart raced, thinking that perhaps Mrs. Williams had come to visit. But as soon as I reached the living room door, I realized it wasn't her at all. Instead, the sound of a boy's voice filtered through the open doorway.

Viv turned when I entered. "There you are sweetheart. I was wondering where you were!"

My stomach churned. She had never called me sweetheart before and I didn't like her referring to me in that way at all. It sounded so fake coming from her.

She smiled at the boy on the couch between Ellie and James. Both Robinson kids were watching some cartoon on television. I blinked as the boy got up from his seat and walked over to me. He was very cute looking. His messy brown hair was flicked back at the front. His blue eyes were friendly, and his smile was kind. His front teeth were a little crooked, but I didn't care. No one in this house ever smiled at me. I felt a fluttering sensation explode in my stomach.

"Hey, I'm Zye," he said.

"Hi, I'm Bella," I said back.

Viv turned to James. "James, let's show Zye your room."

Zye pressed his lips together and followed Viv and James upstairs.

When I glanced back at Ellie I caught her glaring at me from the corners of her eyes. I ignored her and went back up the stairs to my room. Slowing down as I reached it, I heard the conversation between Viv, James, and Zye.

"You're not allowed to touch my stuff," James said, and I rolled my eyes.

Zye seemed to be a little older than me so I doubted he would want to touch James' toys.

Closing the door to my bedroom, I sat down at my desk to finish off my homework but my mind wandered to Zye and I wondered where he had come from. He was obviously another foster kid, so we had that in common. But I didn't see him again until we all sat down for dinner. And although he'd seemed friendly earlier, he had since become sullen and quiet.

At dinner, Max kept his barking tone to a minimum, but he never bothered to talk to Zye at all. In fact, Max showed very little interest in anything except the food on his plate and having quiet kids at the table.

Zye did everything that Viv asked of him without a word. I caught Ellie constantly watching him and when she realized I'd caught her out, she blushed a little and looked away. She then directed mean glances at me instead.

Just as I had on my first night, Zye picked at his food but ate very little. After dinner, Viv sent him upstairs to shower. She then ordered Ellie, James and I to clean up the table.

It wasn't until the following morning that I saw Zye again. When Ellie and James took off out the door for school, I stuck with Zye and walked alongside him, desperate to have someone to talk to. He was in the same situation as me and I hoped we could get along.

"Are you nervous about going to a new school?" I asked him.

He shrugged. "Not really."

"I was," I admitted. "My first day here wasn't easy."

"The first day is the hardest at any new school."

"How many schools have you been to?" I asked.

He laughed. "A lot."

"Well, I'm sure you'll do fine," I said. "You can hang out with my new friends and me if you'd like."

He grinned, showing a dimple on one side of his face. "Sure."

I wanted to know everything about him, but I didn't want to appear nosey by asking a heap of personal questions. So, instead, I talked about school. I'd always been a pretty good student but I learned that he struggled with a lot of subjects.

"I hate English and writing the most," he shook his

head. "I'm so bad at it!"

"We can always do homework together," I said, "if you want to that is. English is my best subject and I'm happy to help."

Even though he was a grade above me, it was my chance to spend some time with someone who wasn't constantly mean to me.

"I'd like that," he smiled.

When we reached the school, I pointed him in the direction of the front office. Since Ellie and I weren't in his classes, he needed someone else to show him around.

I then met up with Olivia whose locker was situated close to mine. As we walked to class together, I spotted Zye with another boy, and he waved at me as they passed.

"Who's that?" Olivia asked.

"The new foster kid staying with the Robinsons," I told her.

"He's so cute looking!" Olivia squealed.

Olivia stared after him and then grinned back at me. I giggled along with her as she asked me endless questions wanting to know all about him. But so far, I knew very little and promised I'd fill her in as soon as I knew him better.

As I entered my classroom, I noticed Ellie giving me her usual death stare. For once though, I didn't care. Instead, I looked forward to the afternoon when I could walk home with Zye.

Over the next few days, Zye and I became closer. He lost his shyness around me, and we did homework together on the back porch every single afternoon until dinner time. On a few occasions, Ellie asked Zye to watch television with her, but he always turned her down. He didn't show any interest in her at all.

I knew she was jealous that the cute foster boy wanted to hang out with me and not her, but it was her attitude that pushed everyone away. She was rude and annoying. Everyone saw it, including Zye. And I didn't blame him for not wanting anything to do with her.

She wasn't used to not getting her way, and I could see she was growing more and more jealous of me. She constantly gave me mean looks and even went as far as to *accidentally* spill her drink all over me.

"Oohhh, *sorryyyy*," she said, locking her eyes on mine and raising her eyebrows. "It looks like your shirt is ruined. *What a shame!*"

I looked down at the bright red stains covering the front of my white t-shirt. There was no way I would ever get those stains out. If my mom was around, she'd probably soak it for me, but I knew Viv would never go to that trouble. And besides, the cheap laundry detergent she used wouldn't be strong enough to remove the stains anyway.

Sighing angrily, I went upstairs to change, consoling myself with the fact that at least I now had Zye on my side. Even with Ellie's constant bullying, things had become so much easier to deal with since Zye had arrived.

It was his background that troubled me though. And I struggled to come to terms with what he'd previously experienced. This was his fourth foster home. I couldn't comprehend what that must be like. When I asked him why he'd moved so much, he simply shrugged and told me that the other homes just hadn't worked out.

It made me wonder if it was easy to be relocated and whether I might also have that option. Although with Zye at the Robinsons, I no longer felt the urgent need to get escape. I was now able to cope, as long as Zye was there too.

At school, Zye made some friends in his own class but he was still friendly when he saw me and always waved at me in the hallways. Olivia and the others were extremely curious about him, and constantly asked me questions.

"He's so cute," Olivia repeated one lunch break, a couple of days after his arrival. "What's he like?"

"He's nice," I said, biting into my sandwich. With the money Viv gave me, I was able to spend a little more at lunch, filling myself up so I wouldn't have to eat as much of Viv's terrible cooking.

"You're so lucky to have him living in the same house as you," Maddie grinned.

I smiled back. I knew I was lucky.

"At least you don't have to put up with just having Ellie around!"

"Oh my gosh, how can you stand living with her?" Olivia shook her head.

"It's not easy," I said, staring at my plate.

Everyone thought of Ellie as mean and annoying. And she deserved that reputation. If anyone did anything wrong, she would immediately run to the teacher…

"Miss Harmon, he did this…"

"Miss Harmon, she did that…"

"Miss Harmon, they're being mean to me…."

I had no idea how Miss Harmon put up with her constant moaning and complaining. Ellie stirred up so much trouble at school that it was easy to see why she only had one friend.

Olivia and Maddie went on and on about her, but I focused on eating my sandwich. Just because I agreed with them, didn't mean I had to add to it. Although, it did make me feel better to know that I wasn't the only one who disliked her so much.

Glancing across the cafeteria, I spotted Zye. Our eyes met, and he smiled at me.

My heart squeezed, and I barely heard the voices of the girls around me as I smiled back at him.

CHAPTER SIXTEEN

As the days passed, Zye and I become even closer. Being foster kids had brought us together. Not many kids knew what it was like to lose both parents, so I was able to confide in him about more of my feelings than I'd been able to with anyone else, including Abbie and Sarah.

At the same time though, Ellie's bullying became worse. Anytime I was forced to be around her, she accused me of doing something wrong. And she made sure it happened when Viv was nearby.

One night at the dinner table, she complained that I'd been sneaking around her room and touching her things.

"Why would I go into your room? I don't even care about your stupid stuff!" I was tired of her lying about me, and I wished Viv would stop taking her side.

"There's no need to speak like that," Viv said, handing out scoops of mac and cheese to everyone. "What's going on anyway, Bella? You know the rules about going into other people's rooms. It sounds like you're becoming a real troublemaker!"

"Ellie's lying," Zye said, defending me. "She's making it all up."

Max slammed his fork down on the table. "That's enough! I will not listen to you call my daughter a liar. If anyone is lying here, that would have to be you!"

"I'm not a liar. Those two are the liars!" Zye pointed across the table at Ellie and James.

I cringed, knowing where this was going to go. Zye had been quiet initially, but as soon as he'd become a little more comfortable, he and Max had begun arguing. James complained numerous times about his toys being out of place, and Max had taken it upon himself to confront Zye, resulting in shouting matches that I heard behind my closed door.

I felt so sorry for Zye having to share a bedroom with an annoying kid like James. Unlike me though, Zye wasn't afraid to stand up for himself.

I watched Max's face scrunch up, and my stomach twisted into a sickening knot. His face always took on that appearance before he really blew up. From the corner of my eye, I saw him shove his chair back and get to his feet. He pressed his hands firmly on the table as he stood, the table legs screeching on the floorboards as they scraped across the floor.

"You close your mouth right now, or I'll do it for you." Max pointed his finger at Zye.

Zye glared defiantly back at him.

"Max," Viv warned. "Sit down."

"I will not tolerate a little snake like him speaking to me like that in my house," Max yelled. His entire face was scrunched up in rage.

My stomach flip-flopped and I fisted my hands in my lap, wishing the yelling would stop.

Zye touched my shoulder and mouthed the words, "I'm sorry," before running out of the room.

The front door opened and closed. I heard Zye's footsteps on the porch before they disappeared for good.

"Where's he going?" Max asked and rushed out of the room. I heard the front door swing open as he yelled out loudly, "You get back here!"

Viv followed him to the front yard and called for Zye.

Shoving my chair away from me, I ran across the room toward the windows. Peering outside, I could see the sun setting in the distance. But there was no sign of Zye anywhere.

Max and Viv argued in the yard then Viv pulled out her cell phone.

Ellie and James continued to eat their dinner as if nothing had happened.

I couldn't help but keep my eyes glued to the doorway, hoping that Zye would walk back into the house at any moment.

When Viv and Max returned to the table, Viv told me to sit down and eat.

"Where's Zye?" I asked.

"He'll be back," Max said. "Now eat, all of you!"

Max didn't comment when I kept my hands in my lap and refused to eat anything more. He'd already scared off one foster kid. I doubted he wanted to do it to another.

I'd never run away since I had nowhere to go. But then neither did Zye. He'd told me that his parents had abandoned him long ago. After separating from his dad, his mother couldn't cope on her own and a year later she gave him up to foster care. He hadn't heard from her since. And he had no idea where his dad was either. I knew he had nowhere to run to. So where had he gone?

I kept looking towards the door, hoping to see his

face appear. But even when I was ready for bed, he still hadn't returned.

Pulling the covers over me, I prayed that he was okay. It was still cold at night and Zye had only been wearing a t-shirt and jeans when he left.

I fell asleep with his face in my head and my hope for his safety in my heart.

The next morning when I opened my eyes, my first thought was of Zye. I jumped out of bed and opened my bedroom door. James' door was still closed so I gently pushed it open, hoping to peek inside and find Zye asleep in bed. Instead, all I saw was James. Zye's bed was empty.

I waited for everyone to finally appear downstairs for breakfast. "Did Zye come back last night?" I asked Viv.

"No," she said, rubbing her eyes. It didn't look like she'd managed to get much sleep.

"He's so dramatic," Ellie said. "But he's not the first runaway we've had."

Runaway? I knew he had run off, but surely he hadn't left for good. For a moment time stood still as I recalled his whispered apology in my ear before he raced out the door. Is that why he said sorry to me? Did he know he wasn't coming back? Was he apologizing for leaving me to face the Robinsons on my own?

The sinking sensation in my stomach made me ill. What if I never saw him again? What if I was doomed to live with the Robinsons without him?

CHAPTER SEVENTEEN

I shuffled around the house all day and did all the chores that Ellie and Viv barked at me. Even when Ellie tried to blame me for chipping her favorite cup, I stood there silently while Viv gave me a lecture on how to treat other people's property. If only she realized the person who needed that lesson was her daughter, the girl who was standing alongside me with her arms crossed and a stupid smirk on her face.

That night, I cleaned up the sodden bathroom yet again, before using it myself. Then I proceeded to stay in the shower for exactly ten minutes by setting the timer on my phone. I was determined to use up my maximum limit and when I finished, I noticed that the hot water had started to cool. Smiling to myself, I hoped there was no hot water left for Ellie when she showered after me.

It was a childish thing to do, but it made me feel a little better. As far as I was concerned, Ellie deserved a lot worse than that. She was a terrible person, just like the rest of her family. And the longer I lived with them, the more I resented them all.

When I returned to my bedroom, I heard the ringing of my phone and raced to answer it, spotting Sarah's name on the screen. I was overjoyed at the sight of her familiar face. Zye still hadn't appeared, so her call was just what I needed.

"I've got some good news, Bella," she beamed. "I managed to get authorization from Mrs. Williams to see you. Tomorrow we're taking you out for the whole day!"

"You are?" I gasped, a wild excitement rising inside me.

"Yes!" she said

"Oh my gosh, that's the best news ever. I can't wait to see you!"

"I can't wait to see you too, Bella!" Mia's little voice chirped happily in the background.

I beamed back as Mia prattled on, my excitement rising at the thought of spending the following day with them. It couldn't come quickly enough.

When I eventually hung up, I felt lighter than I had in a long time. A day out with Sarah and her children…I didn't care where we went or what we did, as long as I was with them. And as I lay in bed thinking about the day ahead, I wondered if telling Sarah about everything that had happened would make it possible for me to leave this place.

So far, I hadn't told her how miserable I was. She felt bad enough about me living in a foster home and it wasn't fair to make her feel worse. But if I shared the truth about the Robinsons and the way they treated foster kids, maybe Sarah would manage to convince Mrs. Williams that her cramped apartment was a much better option for me after all.

It was my only hope. I'd had no contact with Mrs. Williams and it was obvious she'd dumped me here thinking I was in the best of hands. I was now a foster kid who she didn't have to worry about. But what about Zye? Did she even know or care about what had happened to him? When I'd questioned Viv about it, she said she'd filed a report and it was all she could do.

"This place isn't a prison," she frowned at me. "And we can't make him stay here. If he'd prefer to live on the streets than to have a caring family look after him, then that's his choice."

I stared at her speechless as I struggled to keep my mouth closed and not tell her what I really thought.

A caring family? She and Max had no idea what those words meant. As much as I missed Zye, I could hardly blame him for taking off the way he had.

Perhaps he really was better off.

The next morning, I woke at the same time as I did every day for school. I wanted to be sure I was ready when Sarah, Mia, and Matthew arrived. I didn't want to waste a moment of our time together and quickly cleaned my teeth and dressed in my favorite outfit. It was a dress my mom had bought for me when we last went shopping together. It helped me to feel closer to her and today was a special occasion. As well, I knew she'd be pleased I was wearing it.

Sarah had said they'd come early and take me out for breakfast. This was the biggest treat and I looked forward to having something other than tasteless, sugary cereal. I kept an eye on the front window as I waited and when I saw Sarah's car pull into the driveway, I ran out to the porch to meet her.

She raced up the front steps and scooped me into a tight hug. "Hey, Little Bean."

Her hair tickled my face but I didn't care. Hugging her was wonderful and a warm feeling worked its way through to my heart.

Tears sprung to my eyes. "Let's get out of here."

She held me at arm's length. "I have to speak with Mrs. Robinson first. That was part of the arrangement."

I sighed and led her inside.

After showing her through the downstairs section of the house, I turned and noticed her expression. I could tell she felt exactly the same way as I had when I'd first arrived. But I didn't defend the house at all. I knew it was in terrible condition and I wanted Sarah to know that as well.

"Where's your room?" she asked.

"Upstairs," I replied.

She nodded. "Matthew and Mia are waiting in the car, otherwise I'd ask you to show it to me."

Viv suddenly appeared and without a word, stared openly at Sarah.

Sarah moved in front of me. "Hello, I'm Sarah Barnes. We spoke on the phone."

Viv walked towards us, pulling her robe around her as her slippers shuffled over the surface of the floor. There was no sign of Ellie or James who were probably still asleep. Max was nowhere to be seen either.

"So you're Sarah?" Viv said, looking Sarah up and down.

"I am," Sarah smiled broadly. To some, it might have

seemed a friendly gesture, but I knew better. She had turned on Mom-mode for me, and I couldn't have been more proud.

Viv nodded and brushed her fingers through her hair. She obviously hadn't been prepared to find Sarah in the house. "You need to have her back by five for dinner," she stated firmly, not an ounce of warmth in her tone.

"I was told I'd be able to have her for the whole day," Sarah said.

Viv pursed her lips. My chest tightened. Viv liked having control, and Mrs. Williams had given her that control over me. I wondered if Sarah argued, Viv would demand that I come home even earlier.

"We eat dinner as a family," Viv said to Sarah. Her eyes flashed as if she was daring Sarah to complain.

Sarah was a tough woman, and I knew she would always stick up for me. But in this situation, arguing would not benefit either of us.

"Fine, I will return her at five."

"No later," Viv said, making sure to get in the last word.

Sarah took my hand and led me out of the house.

She chewed on her lip all the way to the car.

"Sarah—"

"Let's get going, we can talk about it later," she said, glancing back towards the house as she opened the passenger side door for me.

Looking out through the window of the car, I saw Viv standing in the doorway, watching us, her face masked with an ugly grimace.

CHAPTER EIGHTEEN

"Bella! Bella!" Mia called from the back seat. I turned and tickled her socked toes. She giggled and laughed.

The sound made me smile.

I tickled Matthew's leg. He tossed his head back and laughed as well.

"I missed you guys," I said, feeling as if I had escaped from jail.

For a moment, I thought about refusing to go back to the Robinsons at the end of the day. Although I knew in my heart exactly what would happen if I did that...I'd be forced to return whether I wanted to or not and Viv would never allow Sarah to take me out for the day again.

Pushing those thoughts away, I shoved Viv and the others to the back of my mind and focused on enjoying every second with the family I loved.

Sarah got into her seat and started the car. Her eyes narrowed as she navigated out of the driveway. She didn't bother closing the gate as we drove away.

Mia begged me to sing a nursery rhyme with her and then prattled on and on in the same way she always did. I was desperate to talk to Sarah and I had a feeling she was keen to talk to me as well, but I knew it would have to wait until later.

As we drove down the street, I kept a lookout for Zye, wondering where he was and what he was doing. Thankfully, the weather had improved and the days and nights had become a little warmer. Wherever Zye was, I just hoped he was okay.

As well as that, I wanted to see him again.

After breakfast, where I stuffed myself full of pancakes and fresh fruit, we visited a park that Sarah said was well known for its large playground. Matthew and Mia loved to visit any park, but this one was special and it was something for all of us to do together.

To begin with, Sarah asked Matthew to take Mia on one of the slides. She then indicated a nearby bench seat and sat down alongside me. "So, how are things going with the Robinsons?" she asked as soon as the kids were out of earshot.

I shrugged. As much as I was desperate to tell her everything, I didn't want her feeling bad for me.

"I want you to be honest," she said. "When I went into that house this morning, I got a really bad feeling…about the house itself and about Vivian."

I locked eyes with her and took a deep breath. I could tell her that everything was wonderful. I could tell her that they cared about me and treated me well. And I could tell her that Ellie was the perfect foster sister Mrs. Williams had promised she would be.

But if I told her those things, I'd be lying. A tear slipped from my eye and I brushed it away, turning to look in the opposite direction so she wouldn't see me crying.

She put her hand gently on my arm, encouraging me to continue. "It'll help if you talk about it, Bella," she said softly. "And if you tell me everything, then maybe there's something I can do to help."

I looked back at her and sighed. I had to tell her the truth. All of it. I needed to share this terrible burden that I'd kept hidden while pretending everything was okay. But it was not okay. It was the worst.

So I began at the beginning.

I told her about the way they all spoke to me. I told her about my broken iPad. I told her that I was made to clean the dirty bathroom every night and I told her about how mean Ellie was and how she kept taking my things. I told her that instead of doing something about it, Viv accused *me* of being the troublemaker. And I finished with telling her exactly what had happened with Zye.

"I'm really worried about him, Sarah. Max had no reason to threaten him the way he did. They're all so horrible. I don't blame him for running off…"

Throughout the entire story, Sarah listened without saying a word. When I finished, she wrapped an arm around me and pulled me close. "I'm so sorry you've been through all of this, Bella. I just wish you'd told me sooner."

I nodded and wiped at my eyes. Tears flowed freely down my cheeks. I couldn't stop them even if I wanted to. "I didn't want to make you feel bad about not being able to take care of me."

"Don't worry about me," she frowned. "I'm fine. You're the one we have to worry about. And from now on, I want to know everything. Do you understand? You're just as important to me as my own children, do you know that?"

I looked at her and shook my head.

"Well you are!" she insisted hugging me closer. "Your mom was my very best friend and you've always been like a daughter to me. I promise you, Bella, I'll do everything I can to help."

A set of chubby little arms suddenly reached around my shoulders in a huge hug. "Gotcha!" Mia squealed from behind me.

Smiling, I turned around and tickled her.

"You're it!" Matthew laughed, tagging me on the arm before running off through the playground.

I chased after the two of them, the sounds of their squeals instantly lifting my spirits. After catching them both they insisted I hop on the swing. As they took turns to push the swing, their laughter continued, filling me with a warmth and reassurance that I desperately needed.

And when I turned to look at Sarah, I saw the same warmth in her eyes as well.

When lunchtime came around, Sarah suggested we go back to her place for the afternoon. It was almost time for Mia's nap, and it would be a great chance for Sarah and me to spend some time together. She said she'd already downloaded a movie that she knew I'd enjoy and I grinned happily at her suggestion.

Any other girl my age might have preferred to stay out for the whole day, to be taken somewhere special, but Sarah knew me well and was aware of exactly what I needed.

When we reached her apartment, I helped her to make sandwiches for each of us. After we'd eaten, Mia settled down for a nap and Matthew took off to his room to play with his Lego set.

When it was just Sarah and me on the couch with a bowl of popcorn between us, she gave me some unexpected news. "I've started the process of applying for custody so you can stay with us."

"You have?" I asked, my mouth open wide in surprise.

She nodded. But she didn't look as happy as I felt. "It's a very lengthy and complicated process. Because of my financial situation, this small apartment, and not being a blood relative, it'll be very difficult; maybe even impossible. At least that's what Mrs. Williams said to me."

I took her hand. "Thank you for trying, Sarah."

"I'm not done trying yet, Little Bean," she said. "It might take a while, but I'm not going to stop until you're home with me every day. You just have to hang on for a while longer. And you can't give up hope!"

When the movie began, my mind wandered and I found it difficult to focus. Living with Sarah, Matthew, and Mia and going back to my old school was exactly what I'd hoped for. But could Sarah make it happen?

I really didn't know. But as Sarah had said, we couldn't give up hope.

And that was one thing, I was determined never to do.

The last few hours of the afternoon passed by way too quickly. When I watched Sarah buckle Mia and Matthew into the car, it took every ounce of strength inside me not to cry.

Sarah knew I didn't want to go back and tried to cheer me up by telling some funny stories about things Mia had done since I'd left. Somehow, I managed to keep my tears at bay. The last thing I wanted was to upset Sarah's children if they saw me crying.

The ride back to the Robinsons was too quick and when Sarah parked her car in the driveway at 4:58 pm, I couldn't bear to release the lock on my seatbelt.

"Do you really have to go now?" Mia asked.

"Yes," I said, glancing at Sarah.

Her lips were pressed into a thin line as if she were trying not to cry as well.

I got out of the car and opened the door to the backseat. I didn't want Viv to blame Sarah if I was a minute late.

As I hugged Mia, her little fingers curled around my neck, holding me tightly against her. "I don't want you to go, Bella."

I kissed her cheek. "I'll see you soon, Mia."

"When?" she asked. "Why can't you live with us now?"

"Bella has to go, Mia," Sarah said from behind me.

"No!" Mia whined and her little eyes teared up.

I knew if I stayed a moment longer, she was going to cry, and then I wouldn't be able to contain myself any longer.

I gave Matthew a quick hug before hugging and thanking Sarah, and then without looking back, I ran into the house.

Tearing down the hallway, I saw that Ellie, James, and Max were already seated at the dining room table. I was hoping that a miracle had happened and Zye might be there too. But there was no miracle and no Zye.

I passed Viv carrying a casserole dish.

"It's time to eat," she said.

"I'm not hungry!" I shouted and ran up the stairs to my room.

Slamming my door, I threw myself onto my bed and burst into tears.

I half expected Viv to appear, ordering me back downstairs for dinner. But she never came.

I cried until I had nothing left. Then eventually, I fell into a restless sleep.

CHAPTER NINETEEN

I couldn't wait to get to school on Monday morning; anything to escape the Robinsons' home and the constant scowl on each of their faces.

As usual, Ellie and James took off down the street without me.

But I didn't care, I preferred to walk on my own anyway.

Just as I approached the corner, I felt the sudden grip of hands on the back of my shoulders. I squealed loudly and whipped around, my heart thumping wildly. Staring into the unexpected face in front of me, I gasped in shock and surprise.

"Zye!" I shrieked. I was so happy to see him and had to resist the urge to throw my arms around his neck. "What are you doing here? Where have you been? I was so worried about you!" My words spilled out all at once as I tried to settle the racing of my heart.

"Sorry to scare you," he grinned sheepishly.

"Don't worry about that, I'm so happy to see you! But where have you been? I was so worried!" I repeated the questions as the realization that he really was back, sank in.

"I found an abandoned shed to stay in. I couldn't go back after what Max said to me. I-I just couldn't."

There was something in his expression that made me shiver. I knew he had a bad past with other foster families. Were there worse ones out there than the Robinsons? And what had he been through over the past couple of days?

"I'm so glad you're okay," I said.

"I'm alright," he said. "I'm starving though. I figured since I didn't have any food or money that I should come back."

I wasn't sure what Viv or Max was going to say about that, but Zye was their responsibility. They couldn't kick him out, could they?

There were so many questions swirling around in my head, but I didn't want to ruin the moment.

"I was so worried about you," I repeated for the third time.

"I was worried about you, too," he said. "If I leave again, I'm taking you with me."

I smiled, knowing he was just trying to make me feel better.

"I'm going to the house to grab a shower and something to eat," he smiled. "Wish me luck with Viv. I'll see you at school later."

And with that, he took off at a run in the direction I'd come from. Thankfully Max had already left for work. I just hoped Viv would be okay when she saw him.

Although I was reluctant to let him leave my side, I turned and continued on towards the school. And with each step I took, my smile grew wider. Now that Zye was back, perhaps things would start to improve.

Over the next few days, however, fights between Zye and Max were constantly erupting, gradually becoming worse as the days went on. Max yelled at Zye for one reason or another and Viv didn't say anything to her husband. It was as if they both thought Zye deserved to be treated that way.

At school and in the house, Ellie copied her father. He picked on Zye and she found every opportunity to pick on me. Whenever I was "in her way" she purposely barged into me. And I faced daily lectures from Viv about the trouble I was causing for her daughter. Finally, Viv took away my phone, punishing me for 'everything I had done to Ellie.'

When that happened, I couldn't even call Sarah to tell

112

her. I knew she'd try to call me eventually, but meanwhile, I wasn't sure how much more I could take.

There always seemed to be someone yelling at Zye or me. And when we came home from school, we hid in my room to do homework until it was time for dinner.

One night, it got so bad between Max and Zye that I thought Zye was going to run away again. Then, after dinner, he handed me a folded up piece of paper. I knew it was a note of some kind and I shoved it quickly into my back pocket. As soon as I finished helping with the dishes I went to my room to read it.

Let's leave tonight!!!

I had to reread it numerous times before the realization sank in.

He wanted to leave the Robinsons'.

And he wanted me to go with him.

Before Zye's return, I would never have even considered it. But now that my freedom to talk with Sarah and Abbie was taken away, things had become unbearable.

I sat frozen in my spot, my head spinning with indecision.

I had two choices.

I could either stay where I was and be more miserable than ever, or I could leave with Zye at my side and escape this horrible place.

Without another moment's hesitation, I started gathering a few clothes, my money, and my toothbrush and quickly packed them into my backpack. Just as I zipped it closed, there was a quiet knock on my door

I opened it to find Zye staring at me, his eyes wide. "What do you think?"

I took a deep breath as I grabbed hold of my bag, my fingers tightening around the strap.

I nodded firmly. "Let's go!"

***

Find out what happens next in

The Lost Girl – Book 2

Available Now!!

Thank you so much for reading The Lost Girl!

If you could leave a review, I would really appreciate it

Thank you so much!!!!!

Katrina xx

To be kept up to date with all the latest books in every one of my series…

Follow me on Instagram

@katrinakahler

@juliajonesdiary

And please LIKE my Facebook page

www.facebook.com/katrinaauthor

Some more books you may like:

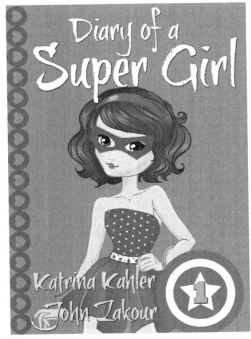

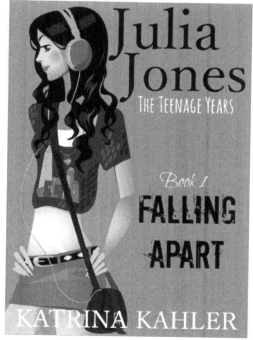

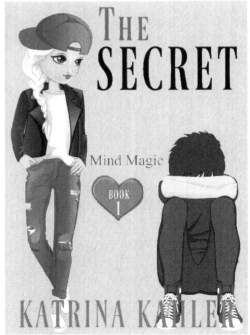

Printed in Great Britain
by Amazon